A WAR FOR MUTANTS

THE GRAND BATTLE

ALBERTO CRUZ PÉREZ

First Paperback Edition, 2025

ISBN 979-8-9883328-2-4 (Paperback Edition)
ISBN 979-8-9883328-3-1 (E-book)

Cover art by Rashed AlAkroka
Edited by Joseph Furmanick
Map design by Yeshmarie Vázquez Cintrón
Character's illustration by Elliott Lugo Lebron

RED ST
VILLA
ART GUN
MAGW
SCA

GREEN DESERT
RASENOF FOREST
RSELA
MIRCORION
CHARCEL

ZENROT

ASTRED

FREDERICK

KEISHLA

*To everyone who believes in a world
for a better place.*

A WAR FOR MUTANTS

THE GRAND BATTLE

CHAPTER
ONE

After the battle that occurred last night in Art Gun's base, Zenrot was struggling to wake up, exhausted from all the fighting and energy wasted in battle. He's taking his time getting out of bed, his eyes opened to the sight of a table with his gear laid out upon it. He sat up on the edge of his bed, rubbing his eyes on the back of his arm before grabbing his watch to check the time. It was 8:48 a.m.

"Shit, I'm late!" Zenrot panicked, hurriedly rushed to the bathroom, brushing his teeth and taking a quick shower. He turns off the water and grabs a towel, drying himself poorly as he walks out near a cabinet searching for his clothes. After getting dressed, he proceeds to wear his armor. "Ryan is definitely going to kill me."

Right in the middle of putting on his armor, he heard a noise at the entrance door—*pam, pam, pam*—someone was knocking.

That's probably the major. I'm so dead!

Zenrot finished fastening the armor as fast as he could,

struggling to put his last boot on. He hopped to the door, almost falling from jumping so fast. When Zenrot reached the door he opened it quickly, already apologizing. "I am so sorry! I overslept and—" he stopped, startled. It wasn't Ryan at the door; it was one of Arashi's bodyguards, wearing his usual heavy body armor.

"Morning, soldier," the bodyguard said bluntly. "General Arashi requests you join him in his office. Follow me, please."

"Um, sure." Zenrot was confused, it wasn't the Major scolding him for being irresponsible with his strict hours. Yet, Zenrot had no choice, the bodyguard went ahead, and he followed. As they walked, Zenrot caught motion out of the corner of his eye. Their cleaner was coming out of room "01." He looked directly at Zenrot. They didn't exchange words, but the cleaner nodded, saying *good luck*.

Zenrot and the bodyguard left the building, walking toward Arashi's office. Zenrot looked around as they walked. There were soldiers marching, vehicles transporting ammunition, and lots of activity. Everyone has been pretty busy and alert after Sentry Run's robots invaded their base. Zenrot was trying to spot Ryan, but he unfortunately was nowhere to be found.

He tried to have a conversation with the bodyguard. "So, any chance you know what this might be about?" Zenrot asked.

The bodyguard remained silent as he continued leading the way to the office.

"The silent treatment… Well, that was awkward," Zenrot whispered to himself. They reached the building and approached the elevator.

"Well, good morning Mr. Zenrot," a voice spoke from behind

them, startling Zenrot. It was Mojo, speaking as he approached.

"Good morning," Zenrot answered, calming himself.

"How's the gun working for you?"

"Pretty well, actually. Thank you for your hard work," Zenrot said politely, knowing that Mojo had done a portion of the work as well.

"Always a pleasure." Mojo slowly stepped closer and closer to Zenrot. "If I can only see just a tiny bit of your energy to see how you—"

"Step aside, scientist," the bodyguard interrupted. "There's a direct order to take him to Arashi, and you're not allowed to get near him."

"Mind your manners, you damn grunt." Mojo glared at him furiously. "I'm the head scientist. Creator of all the advanced weapons that you use to defend yourself! So, learn some respect!" He calmed down a bit and looked back at Zenrot. "If you need anything regarding your new gun, just let me know."

"Thanks," Zenrot said awkwardly. Mojo nodded and backed away, returning to work. The bodyguard signaled Zenrot to keep following. They entered the elevator and arrived at Arashi's office in short order. Zenrot got out of the elevator while gazing at his surroundings. There were soldiers in the room and bodyguards in every corner. Zenrot felt worried that there was trouble. In front of Arashi's desk, there were three other people.

"Sir, he's here," the bodyguard shouted, announcing their arrival.

"Ah, great. He finally arrives," Arashi said pleasantly from across the room. The three people who were in front of him all turned around. Zenrot recognized one as the same woman he'd seen back at the residence, but the other two were unfamiliar. He assumed they were the other two mutants because they were standing next to the girl. "Come, I want you to meet your team." Zenrot's expectations weren't disappointing, they're the MSF. He walked up to the group, focusing on presenting himself professionally. Deep down, he was nervous to be meeting the other mutants for the first time. Zenrot fell into place in line beside them. "Everyone, this is Zenrot… um—" Arashi faded into muttering, certain that Zenrot didn't have—or remember— a last name.

"Zenrot Bellator," he jumped in, finishing the sentence. "Nice to meet you all." Arashi momentarily looked surprised at the mention of his last name, but that quickly changed to a more confident expression as if he remembered the answer—although Zenrot had given himself that last name with Ryan and never mentioned it to Arashi. Despite that, he played along. One of the mutants came closer and greeted himself by stretching out his arm.

"Nice to meet you. My name is Astred Mackol." He had a big presence: both tall and very muscular. Astred was bald, with brown eyes, and probably six feet, five inches tall. From his appearance, he looked to be in his early forties. Astred wore a black t-shirt with Art Gun's logo on the left side of his chest, black and red camouflage pants, and armor from the waist down. He wore no armor from the waist up, and Zenrot thought it was probably because of his huge muscles. He reached out in return and shook hands with Astred.

"You're the one I spoke to on the radio back at the invasion," Zenrot pointed out.

"That's right!" Astred confirmed. "I heard you were the one who had an open path for our reinforcements. That was quite a show you gave with that energy blast."

"*Hehe…* Thanks," he said nervously, yet flattered.

The second mutant approaches Zenrot.

"My name is Frederick Crossvelt," he introduced himself, "but you can call me Freddy." Zenrot took a quick look at Freddy. He was shorter than Astred, just an inch under six feet tall, and looked to be about the same age as Zenrot. His voice, confident and firm, sounded older. He wore the same gear as Zenrot.

"Nice to meet you Fred—" As he saluted him, he noticed Freddy's curly hair looked like it had been on fire; there was smoke and ash coming out of his hair. Zenrot also noticed his eyes weren't a common color, either—they were neon orange. *Damn, glad I'm not alone with this one!* Zenrot thought. He asked politely if something had burned his hair, and Freddy started laughing.

He explained that was his natural hair; his abilities were related to fire. Zenrot also noticed a scythe on his back. The staff portion was about five feet long, and the blade had an interesting shape with a curve that grew thicker as it reached the staff.

"I also heard you were the one who created the fireshield around the base. Thank you for the hard work to protect everyone you could," Zenrot said with generosity.

"No need. It's part of the job. I'm the one who should be grateful. You saved our asses with the reinforcements."

Zenrot finished talking with Freddy and turned to the woman he saw before.

"Hello there," he said politely. "Nice to meet you, miss." She had a serious face and didn't say a word to him, only staring at the hand he was offering for her to shake. Her hair was black and tied up in a ponytail with two sticks. She had almost the same gear as Zenrot and Freddy, but with the addition of a custom backpack with daggers sheathed in it on her back.

"This is the other member?" she asked, visibly disappointed. Zenrot lowered his hand because he knew with that question that she wouldn't be shaking it.

"That's Keishla Monulen," Freddy said on her behalf. "Forgive her, she's suspicious of working with someone she doesn't know."

"You don't need to tell him my full name, Frederick!" Keishla shouted fiercely.

"And quite an attitude as well," Zenrot said, whispering sarcastically.

"Got a problem, Dark Boy?"

"Oh, no problem at all." *Dark Boy? That's a new nickname.* Zenrot thought, and he rolled his eyes to emphasize the sarcasm. "But I think someone needs some manners around here," he said while walking away to avoid her. Freddy covered his mouth to prevent himself from laughing out loud.

"Why you little—"

"Alright. Now that we're all here together," Arashi interrupted, bringing them back to the subject, "please form a line standing next to each other." To maintain their distance,

Keishla stood next to Freddy as Zenrot moved next to Astred. "As I recall," Arashi continued, "each one of you has finished all the training we can offer here at Art Gun. Not to mention that you were the strongest mutants who stood themselves in the invasion… It is finally time for all four of you to work together as a team. You are the only mutants qualified enough to battle outside these walls. Each one of you has unique abilities, and you will use them to aid our men and fight to save anyone who Sentry Run tries to eliminate."

"Even if that's true," Astred replied while crossing his arms, "this isn't exactly why we're here, right? You've been fighting against Sentry Run for years, and I know you've worked hard to gather as many mutants as you possibly can. So, what exactly are *we* doing here?"

"Always finding the loophole, eh, Astred?" Arashi said as he smirked.

"Just mentioning the facts."

"Well then, I'll cut to the chase." His voice changed. "We've been trying to attack Sentry Run's headquarters directly to end this war once and for all." All four of them opened their eyes, surprised. "The reason my crew has been working crazy over these last few months was because they have been working on engagement strategies, and analyzing their defenses and what weapons we are up against. They have advanced technology, therefore some of our battles have been hard to win. They've even created robots to fight for them. We need to strike against the enemy before they decide to invade once again."

"Sentry Run's robots have progressed quite a lot," Astred

agreed. "They upgraded their weapons and added verbal communication to their system so they can interact with Sentry Run's soldiers in the battlefield. Not to mention they have scanners to identify what type of enemy they are facing. That is if you're in their sight, of course."

"So what?" Keishla sounded annoyed. "We have been falling back because some cables and bolts are fighting now. How hard can it be?" She sounded confident, but Astred gestured with his finger on his lips. He mouthed for her to *shush it* and she stayed silent.

"If it was an easy task, more mutants would be standing here instead of just the four of you," Arashi clarified while Keishla seemed ashamed. "Besides, since the first invasion of the Spartans we lost countless people—especially mutants. It's been hard to recruit more since then."

"So, what's the plan?" Astred asked.

"Our plan is for the four of you to clear any city or village Sentry Run has invaded and rescue any civilians in their captivity. Starting with a small population and moving to a bigger one. The MSF will be the frontline. Of course, you won't be alone. I'll send soldiers to back you up in battle. That way, word will come around and Sentry Run will have no choice but to send their best robots to fight against you. When that happens, an army of Art Gun soldiers will wait for them to arrive and ambush. Meanwhile, the MSF and other squads will attack directly at Sentry Run's headquarters."

"Sounds like a plan, but how do we know when it is safe for us to engage? I mean, even if you manage to force them to release a strong army, won't there be other robots for massive security? You said they have advanced technology, so we will probably have a lot to stand against," Zenrot stated.

"Glad you asked about when to engage," Arashi spoke energetically. "You see, I've already sent a few squads during these months. Luckily, some of our men had the chance to hack their security system and—thanks to Astred's intelligence—we now have ideas on how to approach. Their headquarters is on an island called the Green Desert. That's one of their highest territories. In the center of the island, they have a giant building—thirty-stories high. On the twentieth floor, they have a lab where they create all their weaponry and robots. Their main computer network is also there. When the time comes, your mission is to extract every fragment of intel that can prepare our army for battle."

"What about team Alpha, Bravo, Charlie, and Delta from yellow rank?" Astred asked. "Aren't you still working on them?"

"Unfortunately, most died during their investigations. We've lost every soldier from that rank. We're in the process of training more recruits. The blue and red teams are fighting in a different section of the battlefield. The green ones are guarding the base."

"I didn't know there's a color ranked system," Zenrot pointed out.

"There are different teams of soldiers," Freddy pointed out, "and the color ranked system is to identify their level. The rank colors are in order: yellow, green, blue, orange, and red. That order goes from the lowest rank to highest. Each color has four different teams: Alpha, Bravo, Charlie, and Delta."

"I see…" Zenrot answered.

"However," Astred joined the conversation, "there's a special team that's not from the color ranks. They go by shadow squad. They are members qualified enough to do the impossible when needed."

"If I may ask," Zenrot said lightly and afraid of the answer, "what team saved me back in Scateror?"

"That was a bravo team from yellow rank. They were the first we sent to search the island. Sadly, none made it out alive. We have been preparing recruits for replacement, but sadly, the more we recruit, the more people keep dying in battle," Arashi said with sadness in his voice.

Wait! So that means… Brandolf is gone? His face turned sorrowful, knowing a friend died. He lowered his face, as he looked to the ground. Keishla gazed at Zenrot, not changing her careless expression but noticing his clenched fist and deducing that someone Zenrot cared for had died. Keishla didn't truly care about his status, but she noticed.

Zenrot looked up to Arashi.

"When can we start helping?" There was fresh confidence and determination in his voice.

"Tomorrow," Arashi answered. "Today, I want the four of you to take the day off. Get to know each other and what you are going to work with. From this day forward, like it or not, you will be like a family working together. No one else will join this team. Do you understand?" Everyone understood the message, but Zenrot believed family was the wrong term to describe them. Astred looked calm but serious at the same time. Freddy looked like a chill, goofy guy. And Keishla continued to look like she hated the world. It would be a strange team. "The leader of this team will be Astred," Arashi continued, "as he's been in Art Gun the longest time and has a lot of battlefield experience. So, everything he says, you listen to. Understood?"

"Yes, sir!" Zenrot, Keishla, and Freddy shouted.

"You are dismissed." Everyone turned around to leave. "Oh, I almost forgot," Arashi called out, stopping the team, "I want you to know that if something happens to Astred, Zenrot is the second-in-command. So, you do as he says when Astred isn't around in the field. Understood?" Zenrot was shocked and surprised at hearing he was the second-in-command. He'd never been a leader, nor did he have real experience in the battlefield aside from the invasions. Why Arashi decided to put Zenrot as second-in-command didn't make sense.

"Understood, sir," Freddy said. He poked Zenrot a couple of times with his elbow. "Congrats, mini-chief!" he said happily. It seemed he was all right with Arashi's decision.

However, one of them was not pleased. "Are you fucking kidding me?" Keishla spoke in a harsh tone.

"Watch your language, Keishla," Astred raised his voice.

She turns to face Arashi.

"Sir, with all due respect, Dark Boy has been in Art Gun less time than Frederick or even me. Why the hell would you give such a responsibility to him?" her arm snapped out, pointing straight at Zenrot.

"With his training and performance during the last invasion, Zenrot has proven he's capable of leadership. I have trust he will keep everyone safe and guide you well."

"This is insane! If someone should be second-in-command, it should be Frederick. Please don't make this damn decision!" Keishla shouted, growing louder and louder in trying to convince Arashi. Astred had enough of her and told her to shut up and have some respect and dignity for Arashi's decision. Keishla was furious and stormed to the elevator without a word.

"Hey, wait up!" Freddy followed her and both left on the elevator. Astred apologized for her behavior and reassured Arashi he would talk to Keishla. Astred took a quick look at Zenrot, giving a soft smile and putting his hand on Zenrot's shoulder.

"I know you will do well, Zenrot," he said, passively congratulating him for second-in-command. Astred's expression matched; he appeared well convinced that he'd do a good job, while Zenrot continued to overthink it. "I must go and talk with Keishla. I'll see you in a bit. Excuse me, gentlemen." Astred said his farewell and walked to the elevator.

Zenrot stood alone, waiting until Astred left the room. As soon as the coast was clear, Zenrot took the opportunity to speak privately.

"General Arashi," he said calmly, "do you think it is the best idea to put me as second-in-command?"

"I don't think, I know," Arashi answered flatly. He took out some files and gestured for Zenrot to look closely. They were the personnel files for each MSF member. Zenrot read over their descriptions and qualifications.

MUTANT 01

Last Name: MACKOL   *First Name: ASTRED*

Date of Birth: APRIL 3, 1924

Date Found: MAY 18, 1942

Abilities: Nanomachines and Steel Skin.

Weakness: His veins are exposed when he uses his abilities; this makes it easy to cut them off.

Additional Description: Abnormal technological knowledge, can craft objects using the environment around him

MUTANT 02

Last Name: CROSSVELT   *First Name: FREDERICK*

Date of Birth: OCTOBER 6, 1947

Date Found: JANUARY 18, 1953

Abilities: Casts fire and manipulates it to his whims.

Weakness: Cold temperatures.

Additional Description: He connects his energy aura with his scythe (via an unknown method). It's as if the scythe and Frederick share the same mind. However, he's routinely overconfident against unknown threats.

MUTANT 03

Last Name: MONULEN   First Name: KEISHLA

Date of Birth: MARCH 13, 1948

Date Found: JUNE 15, 1960

Abilities: Telekinesis and Speed

Weakness: Can't lift a heavy object with telekinesis, Difficulty controlling her aura.

Additional Description: Can kill silently and shoot long distances without ever missing a target. Prefers daggers and swords. Difficulty communicating but follows orders.

Zenrot took the opportunity to learn what each member was capable of. Reading their descriptions, he could understand why Arashi picked him as second-in-command. Arashi then brought out the last file, scribbled some details on it with a pen, and handed it over. It was Zenrot's file.

MUTANT 04

Last Name: **BELLATOR**   *First Name: ZENROT*

Date of Birth: UNKNOWN

Date Found: JUNE 15, 1965

Abilities: Super strength and releases dark violet aura.

Weakness: Difficulty controlling and releasing aura.

Additional Description: Can lift the weight of a mountain. Still in process of discovering his abilities; was given a special weapon (The Energy Assimilator) to control his aura. Has proven his leadership skills and respect for others.

Arashi took back the files and stored them in a folder.

"So you see, my boy, I have high hopes for you. I know it will be hard, but I also know you'll manage." One of his bodyguards walks closer and whispers in Arashi's ear. By his expression, it looked like he remembered something important. "I would love to keep talking, but I have things to discuss about our next attack."

"Of course, sir. Thank you for your time." Zenrot turned around to leave, then paused. "By the way, general… Do you know where Major Ryan might be?"

"He's been sent on a special mission to guide a group of troops in battle. He won't be around here anytime soon."

"I see… Any chance you know how long it will take them to come back?"

"Hard to say. Remember, we're at war, my boy. Anything can happen. Now you go and enjoy this day off. Take this opportunity to know your team better. It is important to gain trust in times like these."

"Understood. Thank you, general." Zenrot said his goodbye and headed to the elevator. Inside, Zenrot wondered why Ryan didn't leave a note if he wouldn't be around for some time. He was worried about the major's wellbeing. Hopefully, he would come back alive. Hopefully, he would see the man that guided him again and be able to introduce his new team. He smiled, knowing Ryan could surely take care of himself.

He will come back, Zenrot hoped.

CHAPTER
TWO

Zenrot reached the first floor, when the elevator's door opened, he walked outside to see Astred talking with Keishla. Zenrot could tell she wasn't pleased, and noticed she was just listening to Astred—it was only a matter of time until Keishla exploded in rage.

Astred's gaze wandered and he noticed Zenrot's presence.

"Ah, you're here," he said gladly.

"Yeah sorry, I was discussing a few things with the general."

"No worries. Say… have you heard of Art's Grill?"

"Yeah, I ate there a few times."

"Perfect. I thought it might be perfect for the four of us to eat together and get to know each other a bit more. My treat," Astred suggested.

"Sounds good to me, because I'm hungry!" Freddy said while rubbing his stomach.

"Sure, we can go there," Zenrot agreed as he followed Astred and Freddy. Keishla stood behind, obviously not planning to go with them. Astred noticed her gesture, however, and insisted she join the team. She followed, an unpleasant look on her face, and silent all the way to the restaurant.

Upon finally reaching Art's Grill, the team stepped inside and noticed the place was quite full. Zenrot and the others felt the disturbance their presence caused by the way some people were looking at them. Everyone looked disgusted, probably because there were four mutants together in the same room. It was a clear reminder that some people didn't like to have mutants around, even if they were working toward the same purpose. Astred scanned the restaurant, finding a table for them to sit together at. Some people even moved from their spots to an empty table to give the message they were not welcome.

"Perhaps we should go somewhere else," Zenrot suggested.

"Astred?" someone shouted out of excitement and ran closer.

"Mr. Han?" Astred recognized the voice and was visibly relieved to hear a friend.

"How have you been? It's been a long time," the old man said, excited at his arrival.

"Indeed, my good friend."

Mr. Han tilted his head and noticed that Zenrot was with him.

"I see you two know each other." He pointed at one, then the other.

Astred informed him that they were assigned to the same team, and Mr. Han was glad to hear the news. He turned around to find them a table and noticed people were taking up space unnecessarily. He waved his hands in the air at the other customers, signaling them to clear a table for the four mutants. Zenrot and the others hadn't wanted to be rude by disturbing anyone with their presence, but it was clear Mr. Han didn't give a damn—and even went so far as to insist that it would be an honor to serve the MSF.

He escorted them to a table with four chairs. Zenrot sat first and Keishla sat on the other side, away from him. Astred sat in front and Freddy next to Zenrot.

"You want the same old, Astred?" Mr. Han asked.

"Of course," Astred replied.

"Well, Zenrot, it's good you're not wetting my place again this time. You want to make a good impression on your team." Zenrot felt embarrassed, covering his face with his hand.

"HA-HA-HA! The hell happened to you, Zenrot?" Frederick asked, still bursting out of laughter. "Did you piss yourself in the restaurant?"

"No," Zenrot answered flatly. "It's a long story."

"Please, do tell." Keishla spoke with a smile on her face. Her elbow lay on the table, resting her chin in her hand. Zenrot ignored the subject.

"A story for another time," Mr. Han said with a wink at Zenrot. "What would you guys like to eat?"

"Just mashed potatoes with chicken and vegetables on the side, please." Zenrot replied.

"I'll take the same thing, please. Sounds tasty!" Freddy shouted.

"Certainly," Mr. Han said and looked at Keishla. "And what about you, my lady?"

"Not hungry," Keishla answered as she laid back in her chair. Astred gazed at her seriously because he knew she was hungry. Keishla was still mad about the recent reunion.

"She'll have the same as me, steak with fries," Astred ordered for her.

"Very well, sir. And to drink?"

"Three waters and beer please," Astred said politely. Zenrot, Keishla, and Freddy looked at Astred at the same time because he ordered the drinks for them. Astred turned his eyes on his team, "I don't care if you three are old enough, you will drink healthier while I'm around. Plus, I'm paying." Astred looked back at Mr. Han, "Can you bring the drinks first please?"

"Sure thing. I'll get the drinks for you and let you know when your order is ready," Mr. Han said before departing to the kitchen.

While waiting, they took the time to speak with each other. Zenrot wanted to know how they joined Art Gun. Astred explained that, many years ago, he was a young adult living with his mother and younger brother. He said his mom was an ordinary human, but he and his brother were gifted with abilities. In time, Sentry Run reached their homeland. They killed his mother and tried to kidnap his brother, but that his brother had sacrificed himself so Astred could escape and live. Luckily, Art Gun arrived and Arashi found Astred. When Arashi found out about his abilities and intelligence, he decided to recruit Astred as a soldier and engineer. They had worked together for many years.

"Has it been hard to find more mutants as time has passed?"

Zenrot asked curiously. Astred nodded and said that Sentry Run has been getting stronger as Art Gun struggled to find strong mutants. There were more mutants found, but their abilities weren't the kind to be useful in a fight on the front lines.

Zenrot then turned his interest on Freddy, asking the same question as he had to Astred. He opened his mouth, ready to speak, but hesitated. He started to think about his past, admitting after a moment that he could barely remember. The only things he could recall were that he was an orphan and had, at one time, been an explorer searching for treasure. During his journey, Freddy discovered he could touch fire without burning his flesh. That had led to the realization that he could manipulate the strength and intensity of the fire as well. After playing with too much fire at one point, Freddy was told he got dizzy and fainted. The next thing he remembered was laying on a bed in Art Gun's medical center. It sounded strange, but it made sense to Zenrot that Freddy might have fainted using too much of his abilities; that was one of the things Ryan had mentioned in learning to control Zenrot's mutant abilities. He knew the importance of learning the balance for their energy.

He turned his eyes to Keishla but didn't dare to ask anything. She already looked annoyed just by being at the same table. Astred noticed Zenrot's curiosity, though, and followed his gaze to Keishla. He looked back to Zenrot and explained she also couldn't remember much of her past, like Freddy. The only memory she had was that she had a family, but she didn't remember how they looked or what their names were. Every time she thought about it, her memory turned into a fog; it was as if something was blocking her ability to remember. All that she knew for sure was that she woke up in Art Gun's medical center and, during her time on base, she discovered her powers.

Keishla grew irritated.

"What about you?" she snapped at Zenrot, interrupting their conversation. "What's your story? Besides blowing robots into pieces." As she spoke, Mr. Han brought the drinks to the table. When he placed the water cup in front of Zenrot, he just stared at it and didn't say a word.

"Keishla, you don't need to ask so harshly," Astred said, calling her out.

"What? He asked about us and we're trying to get to know each other. So, I just asked him a question."

"Still, you don't need to be—"

"It's all right," Zenrot interrupted. "It's only fair." Zenrot took a deep breath. "When I asked about the team who saved me back at Arashi's office, it was because they found me in the city of Scateror. According to those soldiers, I defeated a Golem, and I was the only survivor."

"You sound like you don't remember anything," Freddy said as a joke.

"That's the funny part," Zenrot said shamelessly, "I don't remember anything about it, nor why I was in that city. The soldiers assumed I had memory loss since they saw my head injured and I lost a good amount of blood."

"It is possible," Astred said evenly, "and it could be that you fought Golems before they found you and were hurt pretty badly."

"Maybe…" Zenrot answered. "Let's hope I remember something in time."

"Bah!" Keishla shouted in disgust as she leaned back in her chair. One arm rested on the table, fingers tapping anxiously. "Sounds like you don't want to speak the truth about yourself." Astred glared at Keishla and she opened her arms, gesturing as if to ask what she had said wrong.

"Believe it or not, I'm telling the truth," Zenrot said firmly, then remembered something else. "By the way… Arashi showed me the documents describing each of you and your abilities. Is there any chance we can discuss how you guys use yours, and I can talk about mine?"

Astred thought it was fair to talk about it before the mission, but it didn't look like it was a good idea at the moment. People were still staring at their table with disgust on their faces.

"Maybe some other time," Astred suggested.

"Yeah… you're right," Zenrot agreed. "Question, do you believe our abilities are a gift, or a curse?"

Before any of the others could answer, the food arrived.

"Order up!" Mr. Han happily delivered the food on to each of them. Freddy didn't waste a second and started eating as if he was starving to death. Keishla surprisingly ate her food with manners.

"Thank you, Mr. Han," Astred said.

"My pleasure! I'll leave you to it. Let me know if you need anything else," Han said before leaving.

Before Astred started eating, he looked at Zenrot.

"In my opinion, it's a privilege to have our special abilities. Yet non-mutants hate us."

"Why is that?" Zenrot asked.

"Have you ever heard the story why mutants are considered dangerous by most people?" Zenrot had heard some story of it a few months ago, but not in detail. He shook his head. "It all began many years ago when a demon invaded our world. Many say he shot thousands of people with his energy. Some were killed during the attack, but others were gifted with abilities."

"What about the circus' story?" When Zenrot asked the question, he noticed the room got awfully quiet. He gazes over his shoulder and sees a few soldiers staring at Zenrrot. He looks back over at Astred.

"Ignore them," Astred said, having the coldest expression while looking at the soldiers. Then he gives a soft smile as he turns his eyes back at Zenrot. "To answer your question, that event was indeed a massacre. According to the reports, the incident happened in a Sentry Run's territory—"

"Wait," Zenrot interrupted. "I thought Sentry Run wanted to eliminate mutants."

"Not at first," Astred clarified, "when Sentry Run started their organization, they were only strict with rules and imprisoned mutants with higher power. However, this mutant in particular went way above with his powers, and killed many lives with one show."

"It doesn't sound intentional."

"Trust me, it was," Astred confirmed. "After that, Sentry Run decided it was best to eliminate mutants. For them it is better to kill a few mutants than rationalize with them."

"Well, that's unfair for the mutants. And you believe all that?" Zenrot asked while eating.

"The demon part, maybe. He did show up many years ago. Yet not many know the actual details. Rumors said he killed thousands of people and is one of the reasons why this whole mess about Sentry Run started. I can't say if he was good or not. I wasn't even born when that happened. But saying the demon is the reason we have these abilities, I say that's bullshit. If my mother was a human and if my father was a demon, my brother and I would have had weird horns on our foreheads like a reindeer." Freddy spit his food out from laughing hard at imagining Astred having horns. Zenrot laughed as well and Keishla actually chuckled softly. Astred was glad to make them all laugh together.

"Now the mutant from the circus, that I believed for sure. That occurred a couple years before Art Gun found me."

"Yet, the other mutants suffer the consequences because of two people," Freddy shouted with his mouth full.

"It is unfortunate… but it shouldn't matter. What we do now as mutants is what defines our future. People can despise us, but we know what is the right thing to do, and I believe you three will go on the good path."

"Well, that's good to hear. Thanks, Astred," Zenrot said in relief.

"Of course." He cleared his plate in a minute and cleaned his mouth with a napkin. "Besides, you're second-in-command now, so I expect good things from you."

Zenrot laughed nervously.

"I'll try my best. I don't know if I will do a good job."

Keishla put her utensils down, not making eye contact.

"Well, maybe you should withdraw."

"Even if I wanted to, I can't. It's Arashi's orders."

"Then you should get the hell out of Art Gun!"

"Keishla, what the hell is the matter with you?" Astred spoke louder.

"I mean seriously, Keishla, don't you see you're overreacting?" Freddy said with his last bite in his mouth.

"I don't know why you guys are all relaxed about the situation. He's spent less time in Art Gun than Freddy or even me! We have experience in the battlefield, we had actual training from professionals, and we *can* control our abilities. Zenrot is still discovering his abilities and was trained by a major who usually trains recruits." It was evident that Keishla had done some digging on Zenrot's record. She knew everything about him. One thing Zenrot didn't like is the way she expressed herself against Ryan; that made Zenrot angry.

"You may say whatever you want about me," Zenrot said, "but show some respect to the major."

"Or what?" Keishla said, provoking him.

"Or I will teach you the manners that you should've learned in your training."

She slammed the table, stood, and gave a dead stare to Zenrot.

"I'd love to see you try!"

"ENOUGH!" Astred screamed furiously, making everyone in the restaurant look. Keishla stormed out of the restaurant, probably heading back to her residence. Mr. Han passed by the table and asked if everything was all right. Astred told him not to worry about it and apologized for all the commotion. Everyone was done eating and ready to leave.

"Again, I am truly sorry," Astred says to Han. "Here," Astred took money out of his pocket. "For the food and a little extra for all the trouble."

"Oh! Please, no need. This one is on the house," Mr. Han says kindly.

"Are you sure?" he asked. "At least let me give you something—for the restaurant."

"Nonsense!" Han shouted. "You guys are the front line of Art Gun now. It's the least I could do to serve you." Mr. Han leaned closer to Astred. "Besides," he whispered, "it's also a little payback to those mean soldiers looking at you disrespectfully."

Astred chuckled. "Very well, thank you, Mr. Han."

"My pleasure. Make sure you come back!"

Astred nodded, shook hands with Mr. Han, and signaled Zenrot and Freddy to head back to their residence and call it a night. Zenrot could tell Astred looked for a way to help everyone, no matter the cause. He not only offered to help at the restaurant, but wanted to take responsibility for Keishla's behavior. Many people back at the restaurant were already unpleasant watching the whole mutant squad together; now everything was worse because of the scene she'd made. Yet Astred looked like he was relaxed, and Freddy acted like nothing had happened.

Zenrot, on the other hand, was bothered by how Keishla had behaved.

"Aren't you guys worried what people will think about us?" Zenrot asked as they walked out of the restaurant.

"Who? Those soldiers back at the restaurant?" Freddy asked, both sarcastic and surprised. "Nah! They can kiss my flaming ass."

Zenrot laughed loudly at Freddy's comment, but not enough to make him forget how Keishla had spoken about Zenrot being the second-in-command.

"Let's be honest, do you think I'm going to do badly for this team?"

"Nah, Keishla is just overreacting," Freddy said, relaxed. "In my opinion, Arashi picked well. I'm honestly not good at leadership and she's not the best choice either."

"Then why make all that drama at the restaurant?"

"Probably because she doesn't know you well," Astred answered.

"I don't understand… I thought the restaurant meeting was to get us to know each other better."

"Yeah, but not everyone trusts easily. Give her time, she'll need friends to trust sooner or later."

"What do you mean?" Zenrot asked as they reached the residence building.

"Hey, Freddy," Astred changed the subject as they stopped at the entrance, "could you give us a minute? I need to clarify a few things with Zenrot before we start working tomorrow."

"Sure!" Freddy laid an arm over Zenrot's shoulders. "Don't be so hard on yourself, mini-chief." Freddy fist bumped Zenrot's chest lightly, then proceeded inside. On the way he passed close to Astred; both raised their arms and lightly clashed them as a gesture saying their goodbye. Astred waited for a couple seconds, then looked around to make sure there was no one else watching them or close enough to listen to their conversation. Astred and Zenrot were finally alone.

"Like Frederick said, don't take it personally. Keishla simply doesn't trust anyone," Astred whispered. "There was a time when medical doctors tried to heal the wounds and scars, but some of them didn't treat her carefully. They patched open wounds aggressively, and when she screamed they would shut her up with anesthesia or simply tie her down. It wasn't because it was needed, but because they looked at her as a pet."

Zenrot lowered his head, feeling a little bit sad for her. "No one did anything about it?"

"No one knew. I found out about it because one of the cleaners at the residence used to work with the medical team." Zenrot realized it was the same thing the cleaner had told him. "It took a while to trust me, and it took time to trust Freddy as well. I know, in time, she'll trust you too."

"Well, must have been a long-ass time, but she seems to respect you."

"Keishla respects me because I've been working with her in difficult situations ever since she arrived at Art Gun. Same goes for Freddy. We're the only mutants fighting for good in these hard times, we need each other. With your help, I have hope there'll be more of us." He puts his hand on Zenrot's shoulder. "So, from the bottom of my heart, please be patient with Keishla. Anything you need, I'm here for you *and* them." Astred winked at Zenrot as a sign of trust, then turned around to go inside. "It's getting late, better get some sleep. Tomorrow is a new journey for all of us."

"Right…" Zenrot followed behind, and both went to their apartments. Astred opened the "01" door and went inside to his room. Zenrot walked ahead to his room and, just before entering, he saw Keishla's "03" door click shut. He got into his bedroom, took off his gear and clothes, showered, and went straight to sleep. He wanted to be rested because the next day, the MSF started their first assignment.

CHAPTER THREE

October 18, 1966

The MSF were at the battlefield escorting Blue Rank: Bravo, Charlie, and Delta to a new town called Magwer where they heard Sentry Run was planning to attack. Three military trucks held fifteen soldiers each. Zenrot, Keishla, Freddy, and Astred were in the first truck. They didn't send many men to engage to see how the MSF team could work together. When they arrived at Magwer, two trucks stopped at a 400-meter distance away from the town and the other, the one containing the MSF, stopped at 100 meters. They opened the back of the truck and the soldiers of the Bravo team positioned themselves in two rows. Astred came out first and took out his binoculars to look around at a distance. He spotted many groups of Sentry Run's armed soldiers, and heavy Golems escorting hostages. The Golems were seven feet tall and made of very thick steel; they looked hard to pierce. Zenrot, Keishla, and Freddy followed behind Astred, waiting for orders.

"Looks like we're going to make some noise," Astred said, lowering his binoculars and turning around. "Keishla, I want you to run as fast as you can and clear every soldier you see in your way, quietly."

She cracked her fingers and neck. "Sure."

"When she gives us the signal, Freddy, you will go and rescue the hostages. Zenrot and I will take care of the Golems. If anything goes wrong, you let me handle the robots, and Zenrot goes with Freddy to make sure no civilians are hurt. Bring them back to safety. Failure is not an option when lives are at stake. Understood?"

Zenrot, Keishla and Freddy nodded, confirming they heard Astred's instructions clearly.

"Once we're out of danger, I'll signal the rest of the troops to come help."

"That won't be necessary," Keishla said before sprinting towards the enemy.

"You'll get used to it," Freddy whispered to Zenrot as they took position to wait for the signal. Zenrot took a deep breath and Astred signaled him to follow and wait in position. They all went into an abandoned building to hide. They climbed to the third story, able to see everything from up there. Zenrot spotted a soldier checking a house for survivors.

A couple of minutes passed, and he started questioning why Keishla wasn't doing her part of the job when a sudden spray of blood erupted from a soldier's throat—a perfect cut that killed him instantly.

"How the hell did that happen?" Zenrot asked. He hadn't

even seen Keishla attack. Watching closely, he spotted a dagger floating in the air following Keishla. Hiding on top of a house, all of her daggers gracefully floated out of her backpack seemingly of their own accord. Telekinesis. So that's her ability.

Keishla looked around, carefully counting every soldier: two on another house, three in front of a vehicle, and the other two walking on the street. She swiftly moved to hide behind a barrel and prepared her daggers near the three soldiers. Zenrot counted five daggers, but then the biggest one split into two, making it a total of six blades. She took a deep breath, aiming at each soldier. The daggers were divided in two groups; half towards the two soldiers alone in the house, and the rest targeting the soldiers standing next to a vehicle. The last dagger split off from the second group, following one of the soldiers patrolling nearby.

Keishla exhaled, and snapped her fingers. Each dagger darted forward, slicing the throat of its designated soldier. She dashed out of her hideout and slipped behind one of the remaining soldiers and twisted his head sharply. The last dagger stabbed the final soldier in the back of his head. Every soldier died and all her knives returned straight to Keishla's backpack. *Ok, I can't lie. That was cool,* Zenrot thought. Keishla raised her arm, moving her hand around in a tight circle.

"That's the signal. Let's go," Astred said. He stood for a moment to prepare his body. His skin was changing into steel, making it hard to injure his body. "Jump now!" Astred jumped and Zenrot followed, both heading down where the Golems were. Enemy soldiers were shouting about being attacked. A Golem detected the threat and gave Astred a heavy blow with a single punch. Astred blocked with his arms, not reacting to any pain. He reversed the block into a grapple and grabbed its arm, flipping the Golem to the asphalt. "Zenrot, now!" he screamed. Zenrot fell from above, slicing the Golem in its center with his sword and destroying it completely. There were four more Golems to take down.

Zenrot took out his gun and charged a small portion of his energy. He shot the Golems to keep the pressure on them. Astred tackled one Golem against the ground and punched it as fast and hard as he could make the robot flat. One was about to ambush Astred, but Zenrot jumped to push the Golem aside. One shot to its chest shut it down.

"Thank you!" Astred said for covering his back. Zenrot nodded, and both continue fighting.

On the other side, the Sentry Run soldiers who were keeping the hostages were so afraid they couldn't find their walkie talkies to call for backup. Before they could do anything, Freddy jumped in.

"Hello, boys." he said, and with one swipe of his scythe, he sliced the soldiers in half. The enemies' uniforms burned from the flaming blade. Reinforcements arrived and soldiers started to shoot at him—and the hostages. Freddy swung his scythe in an arc, creating a round fire shield protecting himself from the bullets by melting them. "This is too easy." He created a ring of fire around the hostages to protect them from being shot as well. While Freddy attacked the soldiers, he became confident he had killed all the reinforcements.

One soldier remained, however, having outsmarted him by

hiding somewhere out of his line of sight. As the Sentry Run soldier aimed at the hostages and just before he was about to pull the trigger—*SLASH!*

Keishla arrived and cut his head clean off.

"You missed one," she said with annoyance. "Next time, look at your surroundings before engaging so irresponsibility."

"Ah, come on. I fought good, right?"

"This isn't a game, Freddy."

"She's right," Astred said as he signaled the Blue Rank squad to engage now that the coast was clear. When Blue Rank arrived, Astred told Freddy to help by making space for the truck. All of the hostages were humans; no signs of a mutant among them. Zenrot was behind the group, carrying Golem parts for supplies and research by Art Gun's scientists. Something started bothering Zenrot and he started examining their surroundings. When they were ready to leave, Keishla noticed Zenrot was missing. He seemed to be zoned out just a few feet away. She walked towards him.

"Hey, Dark Boy!" Keishla called. "We're leaving, you coming or what?" She stepped close to him.

"It's strange," he said in a low voice.

"Strange, what?"

"This was too easy."

"Maybe because they didn't expect us."

"That, or it was a test…"

"Speak, Dark Boy. Come on, we don't have all day." Zenrot followed her and sat inside the truck to head back to Art Gun's base. Keishla forgot what he had been talking about, but he stared thoughtfully at the remains of one of the robots, noticing their glassy red eyes.

There's something odd about these robots, and I can't tell what, he thought on the way.

***

It had been almost three years. The date was May 22, 1969. The MSF, along with other squads, had been going from town to town saving more civilians, but not a single mutant had been discovered. They'd been killed before anyone could save them. Some said Sentry Run had taken the mutants back to their facility, but that didn't make sense for Zenrot and the others. Why would they take mutants if their goal was to eliminate them?

They had, however, discovered that Zenrot was right. The battles were *too easy*. Mojo categorized the different parts inside the Golem's head, finding a video recorder that taped the fight live attached to a transmitter wired into the Golem's head. Sentry Run had proof of how big of a threat the MSF was. They had to work faster.

During those years, Art Gun had been working on a strategy to attack Sentry Run's base and finish the war once and for all. Arashi received intel from someone working underground at Sentry Run headquarters. He discussed their plan with Mojo.

Since the MSF was contributing to the cause by winning the cities back, the enemy had retreated to their base. However, sending men to attack the base directly wasn't the best option: men were dying when they arrived. All had been eliminated, but not by the hands of a human. The informer said Sentry Run had created something to eliminate heavy threats. Sentry Run was focusing more on creating weapons than training humans since they didn't trust in anyone, not even themselves.

Mojo was on a chair in front of Arashi's desk. "We should strike now!" He shouted, jumping out of his chair. "How long will you keep sending men? Until they all die? I thought you had formed the MSF for a reason."

"And I did," Arashi answered calmly.

"Then why not send them already?" Mojo shouted angrily.

"Because I don't want to lose valuable soldiers like the first team of the shadow squad. Which I know you're completely aware of it."

Mojo scoffed and turned his eyes away from making eye contact with Arashi.

"Besides, I'm waiting for intel."

"And that would be what, exactly?" As soon as Mojo finished his sentence, someone came out of the elevator: a messenger, running as fast as he could towards Arashi.

"Ah, you're here. Tell me you got something," Arashi said. The messenger had a file in his hands and gave it to the general. When he started reading, his expression changed. The situation was worse than he thought.

"What is it?" Mojo turn his face while asking, "I don't like that face of yours, it's really rare for you to show fear."

"All this time… no mutants have been found…" Arashi mumbled.

"With all due respect, what's going on?" Mojo said desperately.

"They have collected enough mutants to use their DNA to create a weapon… A weapon that can easily destroy any kind of mutant, no matter the threat." He glanced at the messenger. "Inform the MSF to report to my office, IMMEDIATELY!" The messenger nodded and departed through the elevator.

"Are you insane! Why would you send the MSF? You clearly said this thing can kill any mutant."

"This intel indicates that it's not fully developed, but they're about to finish it. They've been testing it around their headquarters. This could be what killed most of our men." Mojo looked surprised. "That's not all of it. Something went wrong in their headquarters." Arashi revealed the pictures of evidence outside of Sentry Run's headquarters. Both Art Gun and Sentry Run's men were dead, spread outside of a destroyed building. "A rumor has been spreading through the troops; they will not dare to go to their headquarters even if I force them. I believe the MSF is our best option. Besides, they have succeeded in every single mission. I think they're more than ready for this type of situation."

"If you say so, general. And by the way…" He looked at the papers on the desk while raising an eyebrow curiously. "Does this *weapon* have a name?"

Arashi double checked the papers, visibly frightened by this weapon. Mojo had never seen him so scared in all the war so far. The general remained silent for a minute, reviewing the dossier until he finally said, "I believe it is called… Project V."

***

In those years, Zenrot and his team had decimated Sentry Run's troops in a number of cities. Following Magwer, the MSF opted to proceed south because most towns were smaller. Aside from Magwer, they chose not to visit Scateror because it had been destroyed following Art Gun's initial encounter with Zenrot. They headed to Charcel, where they rescued a large number of citizens and were taken back to Art Gun's base. Then they traveled to Mircorion, where all civilians were executed. It appears that most ordinary civilians were hiding the mutants in order to maintain their lives. When Sentry Run learned of the situation, they determined to eliminate every live individual in the city.

Zenrot and his team are able to destroy opposing troops, but Zenrot is upset about the scenario even though they win. Not only did the civilians perish in vain, but Sentry Run only used Golems and Spartans to assault the city. Sentry Run's human soldiers were all absent from the conflict. All MSF members were unsure whether Sentry Run was generating more robots over time, or there were fewer humans inside the organization... or they were simply cowards.

On the same day, May 22, 1969 at 5:46 p.m., the MSF was at another town called Dursela. It was the latest and largest location which Sentry Run had sent a squad to attack. Since Zenrot and the others had won most of the fights, it wasn't necessary to risk many of the men. The Blue Rank Bravo Team had fifteen men scattered across the place searching for survivors. Zenrot sat on the ground with his legs crossed. Astred gathered parts from the destroyed robots while Keishla sat on a nearby boulder. Freddy lay on his back on the ground, his hands behind his head.

"This is getting easier every time, we're a pretty good team after all," Freddy said calmly.

"What's next, Astred?" Keishla asked.

"For now, we wait until the soldiers check the perimeter." Astred ripped a memory unit from one of the robots and wires from another, storing both in his travel pack.

"What's that for?" Zenrot asked curiously.

"Just some silly invention I have back at base."

"Doesn't Arashi demand all useful tools back at the lab for the scientists?" Keishla reminded, since Arashi was always strict with his orders.

"True, but what's the point in giving good materials when we can make something for ourselves?" He winked as a sign of trust, and Keishla and Freddy laughed softly. Zenrot smiled. Astred looked around and whispered to the group, saying, "Remember, we must take care of ourselves as well. You can't trust *everything* they do."

Zenrot was surprised at how he spoke about Art Gun and asked, "You assuming they're up to something?"

"I don't know, but remember not all their methods are the right ones." Just as Astred made his point, a soldier arrived at their location and announced they'd been requested at Arashi's office as soon as possible. They were surprised to be suddenly needed since they had just finished a fight. Something bad must have happened. They went to the truck and headed back to base. After an hour-long journey, Zenrot and the others passed through the Art Gun gates and rushed to Arashi's office as fast as they could. When they arrived, Arashi was sitting on his desk. The MSF fell into formation, making an evenly spaced straight line in front of the general.

"Afternoon, soldiers," Arashi said. "How was the mission?"

"Pretty easy and simple," Freddy said confidently.

"Glad you're finding it easy, because now the real war will begin." They all gasped in surprise. "We have finally had official intel about Sentry Run's headquarters. It appears there's been a breach inside their base."

"What exactly happened?" Zenrot asked. Arashi put a series of pictures on his desk. A building that had thirty stories. Windows broken. Dead soldiers of Art Gun and Sentry Run both. There had been a massacre outside the building.

"What… the… fuck?" Keishla said, shocked by the images.

"My thoughts exactly. We assume something went wrong inside the building."

"What is our mission then?" Astred asked.

"You have two objectives. First, to find their research, blueprints, and any other information we can use against them to figure out Sentry Run's next plan."

"I assume this isn't the hard part, is it?" Zenrot pointed out.

"I'm afraid not. While you guys are looking for the intel, your secondary mission is to destroy the weapon that can destroy anyone—even mutants. It's called, 'Project V.'" That scared them off a little. "Sentry Run was working on a project using mutant DNA to form that weapon. The reason you haven't found any more mutants is because Sentry Run's men beat you to it."

"How come no one told us any of this?" Astred questioned Arashi.

"We just found out from one of the civilians that you guys saved. It was also confirmed by our last intelligence delivery," Arashi answered. Astred couldn't believe it. "In three days, you will be sent to Green Desert Island on a helicopter."

"Just us?" Zenrot asked curiously.

"Correct."

"I thought you were going to send troops alongside us," Astred said in a demanding tone.

"It'll be best if we just send the four of you. We don't want you to worry about your allies while you're on the mission. This is a tough quest, soldier. We can't fail this mission. You must destroy the weapon and recover every piece of intel you can find. This will be the perfect opportunity to finally gain a huge advantage against Sentry Run, once and for all!" Arashi said proudly.

Keishla and Freddy looked like they were convinced by the plan. However, Zenrot was nervous about going just the four of them alone on the mission. Zenrot could tell Astred found something odd about the mission as well. They were given three days to prepare themselves for the mission, then dismissed.

All four went to the lobby but took a detour before leaving the building. Zenrot snapped his fingers, turning to search for Mojo to ask him a few questions about his gun. He found him working at his desk, surrounded by a handful of other scientists. Zenrot approached him, and Astred and the others followed.

Mojo was always busy and always intrigued by new research. He was rushing and yelling to his crew to work faster and smarter. Zenrot raised his hand a little, trying to draw his attention, but Mojo was focused. Keishla didn't want to wait any longer than they had to.

"Yo, baldy!" she shouted, then looked away.

"Who the hell call—Oh, it's you, Zenrot. Forgive me, I thought I heard someone calling me rudely."

"You don't say," Keishla mumbled, setting Freddy laughing. Astred gave them a look meaning, *behave* while Zenrot asked Mojo a few questions about the gun. While they were discussing, Freddy looked around the engineering area to entertain himself while they waited. He noticed a file with his name on top of Mojo's desk. It also had a red stamp that read "SUBJECT 01," which sparked Freddy's curiosity about what was inside the folder. He slowly walked toward Zenrot, faked a slip, and crashed on top of Mojo's desk.

"Damn! Sorry, silly me," he said, making a show of shyly apologizing. "Must have stepped on something with all this work around." Papers had gone flying into the air and Mojo was trying to snatch them all as they fluttered down.

"You imbecile! Be careful. You almost screwed up a lot of work."

As soon as Freddy was going to step back, he slipped the folder off of the desk and hid it behind his back. After looking around to make sure no one had seen him take the file, he crammed it inside his pants.

After a long conversation, Zenrot had the information he needed. A staff member stopped the MSF before they departed, asking for a picture of each one of them to attach to their personnel files. Zenrot and the others followed the man to a photography studio where they took portrait pictures for the soldiers. The photographer set his camera up in front of the white backdrop to compose the shot.

"All right, who wants to go first?" the photographer asked. Astred volunteered and the photographer took two pictures; one standing facing front and the other one facing to the side. Then went Freddy, next Zenrot, and last Keishla. Before they left, Astred went to the photographer and asked if it was okay to take a picture of the four of them together because he wanted a memento.

"Are you serious?" Keishla asked, annoyed.

"Yes, I am," Astred pointed out. "I want each one of us to have a photo we can carry in our pocket."

"Aww, a family photo!" Freddy said, grabbing Keishla's cheeks and mocking her. "Come on, Keishla. Imagine the four mutants, heroes of Art Gun. The ones who made peace between mutants and humans." She punched him in the arm.

"Do we really have to? I hate taking pictures," Keishla said, irritated as they all went to pose in front of the wall. Astred stood behind since he was the tallest. The others stood in front of him in a line: Zenrot, Keishla, and Freddy. The photographer signaled he was taking the picture in five, four, three, two, one… *click.* He took the picture. Before they left, he indicated it'd be ready the next day. They finally left the building, and it was dark. After such a long day, no one wanted anything other than to return to the residence to sleep.

CHAPTER
FOUR

The next morning the sun was hotter than ever. Zenrot was alone at the training field practicing with his sword. Astred said he was working on a few projects with the junk he had recovered from the last mission. Freddy said he wasn't feeling well and stayed in his bedroom. Keishla hadn't answered when he knocked on her door. Zenrot had been out there three hours already, so he took a five-minute break. He sat on the grass with crossed legs, placed his sword aside, and drank a bottle of water. He heard someone approaching from behind.

"Well, you look like you haven't slept all night." He recognized the voice and was surprised at who it was.

Zenrot looked back, "This is a surprise, did something happen, Keishla?"

"Well, I wanted to practice alone but Astred knew you were here and forced me to share the practice field with you," Keishla said with clear annoyance. Despite her tone, she stood next to him and offered her hand to help Zenrot stand up. He accepted it.

Even if they had been working together for years, Zenrot knew she still didn't like being around him.

"Why do you hate me so much?" he asked seriously.

"Because you are *you,*" she said smirking.

"Very funny." His response was blunt. Keishla ignored him completely and headed away to start practicing. Zenrot grabbed her arm, and she looked at him angrier than ever.

"You're lucky your hand is still attached. Take it off."

"Is it because people have treated you badly? I mean, have I treated you bad since I got here? I only see you treating everyone like crap."

"You don't know shit about me!" She released a dagger from her backpack. It floated in the air, the point aiming at Zenrot. He raised his hands, stepping back and trying to communicate that he meant her no harm.

"I know the doctors in the emergency room and at the clinic didn't heal your wounds and scars as they were supposed to," he said softly. "You don't trust them because they harmed you and didn't have any intention of helping you. That's why you prefer to let your wounds heal on their own."

Keishla looked down, silent, but her expression softened.

Zenrot continued. "I don't expect you to be my friend or have any kind of bond, but I want you to give me the chance to earn your trust." After that, she stood for a minute thinking. The dagger slowly went back to her backpack.

She took a deep breath. "Look, I'll be honest with you, and pay attention! You seem like a nice guy, I'll give you that. It takes me a while to trust someone, especially the way everyone behaves around here. I *really* don't trust anyone in the army, some are fucking racists and mean bastards. It took me a long while to trust Freddy, and he's a chill, cocky guy."

"And Astred?" Zenrot asked.

"Astred, well… I don't know, he's not like anyone I've ever met. He always cares for others, no matter who you are or what your background is. Especially if you're a mutant. He sees them like family. I could say he's like a father figure. He's a lovable guy—I can't be mean to Astred. That's why every time he calls me out, I get mad, but I don't answer him. Because he's always looking for the best in everyone. He has full trust in you, too. He hasn't told me personally, but I know he does."

Zenrot felt flattered but quickly changed his perspective and asked, "What about you? Can you trust me?"

"Well… I mean, you're second-in-command on this team. The reason I was bitching about that is because I'm afraid you'll lead Freddy and me to our deaths."

"The last thing I want is to see my comrades die. I'd rather sacrifice myself than let anyone get hurt," he said proudly. For some reason, Keishla knew he meant it. She wanted to tell him they could work together and see if, with time, she could trust Zenrot, but her pride wouldn't let her confess.

"Well, let's see how that goes." Keishla puts her backpack on the ground and starts walking to the field.

"Where are you going?"

"To train. You coming, or what? Let's see what you can do." She walked ten feet further into the field and started a practice fight with Zenrot. He smiled, walking towards her and taking a combat position.

She didn't give me all the answers to my questions... but it's a start, he thought. Then they started to practice fighting.

***

It was 5:56 in the afternoon. Zenrot and Keishla had practiced in the training field for a couple of hours before both headed back to their rooms for a break. Their clothes were dirty and torn; they had gone all out—just like a real battle. Both had the opportunity to learn each other's limits. Some were shown in practice, others they took the time to talk over. As they reached headquarters, Astred was outside talking with Freddy and, by the look on their faces, it wasn't a pleasant chat. They noticed Zenrot and Keishla arrived and changed the subject.

"Finally, you two are getting along," Astred said cheerfully.

"Don't be a fool. He's on our team, might as well know if he's a good fighter."

"Aren't you supposed to know that already?" Freddy pointed out. "I mean we've been together for years—"

"Freddy, one more word comes out of your mouth, and I will seal it for you." They all laughed together. "By the way," she said to Zenrot, "try not to sleep too early today. You don't either, Freddy." Keishla made eye contact with Freddy to make sure they were talking about the same subject. Zenrot was confused and whispered to Astred to ask if he should worry. He chuckled and assured Zenrot not to panic. Keishla insisted Astred should join but he refused because he would be working all night. They went inside the building and Astred went to his room. Just before they went inside their bedrooms, Keishla turned to Zenrot.

"Be outside at 8:00 p.m. If you don't show, don't expect me to trust you so easily. Oh! And no need to bring your weapons." Everyone entered their individual quarters. Zenrot took a shower, put a gray shirt and some brown jeans on, and laid on his bed to wait. He wondered what this was all about, joining Keishla and Freddy outside headquarters. She did mention it was a vote of trust, so that was a start. He waited, periodically checking his watch.

At 7:55 p.m., Zenrot left his room. When Zenrot opened the main door, Freddy was already outside. "Ah, you're here," Freddy said gladly. His hair was subdued, only a small fire at the moment. He was dressed the same as Zenrot. "Keishla hasn't arrived yet, so feel free to wait."

"But wasn't she the one fighting for us to be sharp?"

"Yeah… She's never on time."

"I heard you, Fireworks!" Keishla screamed as she walked through the doors. When she came out, she was wearing the same outfit as they were. Her hair was down, black straight hair that reached her waist. "Well, let's get going!"

"To where?" Zenrot asked.

"You just follow us, Dark Boy. We're heading outside base, so you better keep track." She started sprinting and Freddy followed. Zenrot was left behind and quickly ran towards them. The three of them ran inhumanly fast, passing all the soldiers. None of them noticed their presence, only feeling the wind from their speed. They passed the entrance gate, ran towards a forest, and toward a giant cliff. Keishla climbed the cliff and continued running until there were no trees. Freddy was next, and Zenrot reached it last.

"All right, we're here." They were in a wide-open space with no villages and no soldiers, just nice scenery of the sky and the forest. Keishla laid down on the ground as Freddy gathered branches and stones to build a fire. He made a ring with the stones and placed the branches in the center, igniting them with a snap of his fingers.

Zenrot was walking slowly, curious about the event. "So, what's this about?" he asked Keishla.

"Just a place to chill and relax," she said while looking at the sky. "What? You never got out of the base?"

"Not really."

"Damn, no wonder you're so bored and lost. Geez."

Freddy laughed and gestured at the clearing. "It's just a spot that we can relax in. Talk freely. Enjoy the moment." He shrugged. "Not get shot at for a few minutes."

Keishla rolled her eyes and casually shredded dead leaves off a fallen branch, tossing them into the campfire as the boys sat down on the forest floor. They traded stories of their experiences going through MSF training.

Freddy and Keishla had trained together, with Astred as their mentor. Seeing the confusion on Zenrot's face, she shook her head. "We didn't trust the majors we were given."

Freddy nodded, continuing, "Since Astred had experience, and Arashi had asked us to choose who we wanted in front of everyone, he kind of had no choice."

Zenrot found himself gazing at Keishla, remembering arguing with her about how Ryan wasn't even an actual major who was qualified to train him. That thought rippled into wondering where Ryan was, how his missions must be going. He hoped that his friend was all right.

Keishla noticed that mentioning him had made Zenrot go quiet, and flicked dirt at him to break him out of his reverie. "What's so special about your Major Ryan, anyway?"

His answer was brief, but sincere. He described how Ryan had advocated for him, and how he had woven strict discipline with genuine kindness.

"Is that why you were balling up your fists the day we met—the news about Ryan?"

He shook his head. "No, the first friend I made here. Brandolf. Yellow Battalion. He was in the squad that found me in Scateror. I was upset because Arashi mentioned they'd been wiped out." Zenrot dug at a piece of old tree bark on the ground, then pulverized it between two fingertips. "I really wanted to show him how strong I've gotten. I hope that doesn't happen to Ryan, too."

Keishla almost hid behind a screen of dark hair, her head dropped. Zenrot could almost make out her expression—a mix of shame and chagrin for having mocked him back then, but no contrition.

Freddy broke the awkwardness by directing their attention back to the stars; by counting them. Keishla pointed out the outline of a reindeer, and Zenrot showed them where he saw a flute.

Freddy jumped in, "Wait! I see something too. Right there, over those trees. Looks like… meat."

Zenrot and Keishla both glared at him.

"What? I'm hungry," Freddy said. The three of them started laughing, having the best time of their lives. After the laughter faded, they sat in comfortable silence, admiring how beautiful the stars shone in the dark. They were able to momentarily forget about everything else—the war, the chaos—and simply live in the moment.

"Thanks, guys." Zenrot broke the silence.

"For what?" Freddy asked.

"For bringing me here."

"Well, there are still things I don't like about you at all," Keishla said flatly.

"Oh, come on, Keishla. You're the one who wanted to bring him here."

"Whatever."

Freddy chuckled at her stubbornness, then he confessed that Arashi asked him for a meeting the next day, explaining he would have to be heading back at some point. Zenrot asked if he knew what it was about, but Freddy didn't know. He assumed it must be something about a mission, and Keishla asked if they could join. Unfortunately, they had requested only Freddy's presence. He wasn't even supposed to tell them the news about it, but he figured they would have found out eventually.

Keishla seemed worried something bad would happen to Freddy and tried to insist on joining him. Zenrot told her to relax, but she couldn't because of her hunches about Arashi taking Freddy to a meeting alone. Freddy was not worried about it; he insisted that if anything went wrong, he'd just stand up for himself. Freddy believed he was strong enough to take on anyone.

He changed the subject by talking about the stars. They stared at them for hours. Eventually, they were getting sleepy. Everyone stood up and put out the fire. Zenrot and Freddy were ready to leave.

"Wait!" Keishla shouted. Zenrot and Freddy turned around. "Let this be a night to remember. Many things could happen after the mission. If we survive, we should do this again." Freddy stood in silence because he didn't know how to answer.

"Of course," Zenrot gladly answered, "once this is all over, we will come back here again. That's a promise." Keishla felt relieved knowing someone else believed in something, in the future. She punched Zenrot's arm, then Freddy's.

A strange way to show her appreciation.

"Thanks, Dark Boy. Still hate your guts, though," she said, taking off for the base on her own.

"Consider yourself a lucky man," Freddy said, "only knowing Keishla for a short time and having her tolerate your presence. Now that's something, *trust me!*" Freddy sped back to base with Zenrot following behind. He was flattered to hear Keishla was accepting Zenrot in her own strange way; it was better than nothing. Zenrot only hoped he didn't screw it up.

"Well, let's see how long it lasts," Zenrot said to himself. In two days, their journey on a *real* mission would begin.

CHAPTER
FIVE

May 25, 1969

It was seven in the morning, and the MSF Team was in Arashi's office waiting for orders and receiving the full intel briefing for the mission.

"Well, soldiers, the mission isn't simple. You're about to infiltrate the strongest fortress in the Sentry Run organization—their headquarters. Expect resistance and massive threats. You have two objectives. One, retrieve intel of all their investigations into weapons, armor, or anything that can benefit our unit.

"The second is the most difficult part. Destroy Project V. Is a maximum-level threat for everything we have worked and must be eliminated, regardless of the cost. Once you are done, report back to Art Gun." Arashi gave them each a radio to communicate with each other in case they were separated. As they got ready, Arashi delivered his last message to them. "Remember, you are our last hope to keep our vision alive, that mutants and humans can coexist and fight together as one. Failure isn't an option."

They all had armor covering their arms, chest, and legs except for Astred. Zenrot looked at him and noticed he was examining Zenrot's sword and gun, along with Keishla's weapons. Then Astred walked to Freddy's scythe, looked it up and down, and attached a small device to the staff—right behind the blade.

Zenrot walked over to Astred. "What are you doing?" He asked.

"Just some upgrades for energy sustainment," Astred answered. "Freddy has this bad habit of overdoing his abilities. So, I created a device to help him regulate his energy while he's on the battlefield."

"Oh, that's great!" Zenrot said, "that's what you've been working on all night?"

"More or less," Astred said lamely. "Don't say too much about this to Freddy, though."

"Why is that?"

"You know how cocky he can get. Besides…" Astred said as he looked at Zenrot, "he'll find out eventually." He gave a wink of trust.

Zenrot gave a small laugh. "Noted."

Zenrot went to grab his sword and his revolver. Keishla picked up her custom dagger backpack and attached a sword to her waist. Zenrot didn't know she used a sword until that moment. *She keeps surprising me,* he thought. Freddy, on the other hand, only used his scythe. Astred brought some of his tech support and supplies for the mission. The four of them walked to the helicopter that was waiting to escort them to the drop zone.

"Wait!" Astred shouted at his team.

"What is it?" Zenrot asked, confused.

"I want you to lead the team this time."

"Are you serious?" Zenrot said, shocked.

"I am." Astred answered, certain of his decision. "It's only a matter of time before one day you must make big decisions."

"Still… don't you think it's best if you—"

"All right!" Freddy interrupted, "Mini-chief is guiding us today!" He passed by Zenrot on his way to the helicopter. Zenrot stood stunned. Of all the opportunities he could've been a leader, why did it have to be this mission?

"You better not fuck it up," Keishla whispered into his ear.

Astred passed Zenrot carrying a lot of supplies for the mission. That explained why he chose Zenrot to lead this time; he wanted to focus on hacking Sentry Run's systems while Zenrot guided the others.

Everyone boarded the helicopter. Astred gathers his equipment into a safe place and notices Zenrot was standing behind, nervous. He approached and laid his hand on the younger mutant's shoulder. Astred smiled. His expression clearly communicated what he was trying to say to Zenrot: *you've got this*. Zenrot nodded with certainty and they both climbed inside the helicopter.

Arashi was near the airfield with his hands on his lower back and his bodyguards next to him, watching their departure. On their way, Zenrot studied the specifications of the threats they may encounter. Astred worked on his gadgets. Keishla sharpened her daggers, and Freddy laid against the wall of the helicopter, sleeping until they arrived.

Four hours passed, and the helicopter had reached their destination. It slowly hovered to a landing between the trees, located a few miles away from their target zone. The island was called the Green Desert because of the massive forest covering it. The MSF disembarked the helicopter. Observing a massive, thirty-story tall building. They hid behind the trees where they could see the target location clearly. It would take time to complete the mission with only four of them. Zenrot gathered the team to finalize the plan.

"All right guys, listen up. When we go in, Freddy and Keishla will scout ahead, destroying anything that moves. I'll stay behind to make sure no one ambushes us. While the three of us are fighting to secure the area, Astred will hack their system to find the research labs. Any questions?"

Keishla raised her hand, "Um yes, why do you have to lead? I need a better team player."

"Well, I can let you fight alone and take Freddy with me, so he doesn't die by your hand."

"Hey, I can take care of myself—and others as well. So, don't you mock me!"

Freddy waved his arms up and down interrupting their conversation, "Children, can we please focus on our mission? Astred, how many enemies must we fight on our way inside?"

Astred looked at the description of the mission.

"As I recall, the intel said that there aren't any soldiers. Technically, no one is alive to keep this building running. What killed the soldiers of Art Gun and Sentry Run are unknown. We don't know exactly what we are dealing with besides Project V. Be on your guard."

The MSF rushed to the building's entrance and smashed their way in. Nothing was guarding the place. The main entrance and hallways were clear. Freddy and Keishla went ahead on the first floor while Zenrot followed behind covering their backs. The three of them checked every perimeter until they reached the third floor.

They reported to Astred the area was clear and he reunited with the others, searching for a computer that was wired into the building. After thoroughly inspecting the area, Astred found one on the third floor. He started working to find any extra intel in the system. Some of the data had been corrupted.

Zenrot continued looking around while Astred worked. He found a map on one wall which specified what each floor was dedicated for. Zenrot told Astred the computer mainframe he needed was on the fifteenth floor.

As they ascended the building, they witnessed desks, chairs, and documents of every office were spread everywhere. Blood had been spilled and bodies ripped apart; Zenrot and the others were more guarded than ever. Freddy and Keishla were still in front to watch for resistance, but they only encountered minor traps that Astred could disable without sounding the alarm.

Freddy believed the soldiers were careless with the traps and that was what got them killed, but Zenrot disagreed. It was too basic of a threat for Art Gun's troops. Astred agreed with Zenrot and said he thought that there should be more stuff hidden. After checking every floor, nothing was detected out of the ordinary. They finally reached the fifteenth floor and found the mainframe computer. Astred started working while Zenrot, Keishla, and Freddy were on guard.

Keishla believed there was something strange in the building because, so far, the mission was going smoothly. "Is it me, or has this mission been the easiest one?"

Zenrot was aware that it was very strange; they were already halfway done and no a single threat from an enemy. He had many questions in his head. *What the hell happened in this place?*

Freddy shared another theory: that the previous troops had dealt with most of the enemies, leaving an open path. Freddy had his scythe on hand and Keishla held the handle of her sword while one dagger lazily floated in the air behind her. Getting more and more nervous by the second, Zenrot was aiming with his revolver and checking every perimeter. Astred was taking his time hacking into the system. After almost twenty minutes, he finally announced he'd obtained what he needed.

"Got the location for Project V and discovered what they have been working on. Project V is located on the twentieth floor, and all their weapons and research were left on floor twenty-five," Astred said, relieved.

"See? Too easy." Keishla said, worried.

As soon as Astred disconnected from the computer room, an alarm went off, triggering a lockdown for the headquarters.

"WARNING! MUTANTS DETECTED, ALL PERSONNEL FOLLOW PRESCRIBED EMERGENCY PROCEDURES AND CLEAR THE HALLS," A voice spoke along with the sirens.

Zenrot and Freddy stared at Keishla, "Easy, right?" Both said dryly.

"Oh, shut up! It was about time we got some action," Keishla said while releasing the rest of her daggers from her backpack. An army of war drones was flying toward them; each one had a mini-gun attached to its underside.

Astred quickly packed his stuff and reunited with the team. "These aren't the common enemies we've fought before, be on guard." He sounded agitated as he prepared for battle.

Keishla sprinted toward the drones. Security guns activated from the walls, popping out and taking aim at everyone. A few of the turrets focus on Keishla and started shooting, but her speed was so fast the bullets couldn't keep up. She sliced a couple of the guns off the wall with her daggers, while Zenrot followed behind shooting others with his revolver. War drones blocked their path, obstructing the hallway. Keishla and Zenrot moved out of the way to let Freddy clear the path. He threw his flaming scythe at the drones and sliced them into pieces which burned away. Zenrot took the lead and everyone followed. They traveled on the main stairs since the emergency ones were sealed.

They reached floor sixteen and were running through the hallways looking for the next staircase to proceed to the next floor.

"THREAT REACHING HIGHER GROUND. SECURE YOUR WORKSPACE, COOPERATE WITH SECURITY FORCES, AND USE ANY SHELTER AS NECESSARY!" Another alarm sounded. Doors hidden in the walls slid open. Golems entered the hall from one side while Spartans appeared from the other.

Astred told Zenrot to fight the Golems with him while Keishla and Freddy dealt with the Spartans. The Golems looked different than the ones they had fought before. They were eight feet tall and weighed a great amount of pounds. Their metal seemed more resistant than the older ones as well. Sentry Run had saved these in case of emergency. One Golem was about to punch Zenrot, but he reacted quickly and dashed with his great sword to block it. The blow hit Zenrot hard enough that it still slid him against the wall. Another Golem was on its way to smash Zenrot. Astred got in its way, his hand rapidly turning into nanomachines. He punched the Golem, breaking its chest into several pieces. Astred helped Zenrot to stand by grabbing his hand and both continued fighting.

On the other end of the hall, Keishla and Freddy were fighting the Spartans. They were big robots with a metal shield in one hand and spear in the other. Keishla ran full speed to slay them with her sword. The Spartans united, standing close to each other and using their shields to create a defensive wall. Keishla didn't react in time and impacted hard against the steel wall. She bounced away, rolling across the floor but regaining her feet quickly. Freddy charged his scythe with flaming energy and swung it, throwing the blade of fire at the robots. It struck the wall of defense, melted through the shields, and exploded into the Spartans. Keishla and Freddy turned to look at how Zenrot and Astred were holding up, finding they had already destroyed all the Golems.

Everyone cleared the room and they reached the stairs up to floor seventeen, covered with many Golems and Spartans.

"Everybody stand back." Zenrot took out his revolver and charged his energy to the maximum level. He could feel the barrel expand to its limit. He fired a single shot, an energy blast hurtling down the hallway to the robots. When it touched the first robot a huge explosion happened, chaining across the rest of them. Even the walls start crumbling down.

Zenrot breathed heavily, feeling the tension in his body for having used that much energy at once.

"All right, let's get going," he said to everyone else as he walked to the stairs. Keishla was surprised at Zenrot's ability. She knew he had abilities yet to discover for himself, but didn't expect they could be that strong. In a way, his strength made her feel badly about herself. Freddy noticed her mood and lightly pushed her arm with his.

"Don't worry, you're no different than Zenrot. Both of you have amazing techniques," Freddy said to her.

"Yeah…" she whispered.

They reach the eighteenth floor. Walking the hallway, they entered a spacious room with a heavy vault attached to the right side of the room. Surprisingly, there were no robots or any other items in the area. The room was completely clean. Zenrot stopped walking, curious about that vault. Keishla and Freddy passed him, heading to the stairs for the next floor. Astred stopped next to Zenrot, noticing his interest.

"You got something in mind?" Astred asked.

"Yeah…" Zenrot answered softly before turning to face the others. "Wait," Zenrot shouted, calling for Keishla and Freddy to stop. He wanted to see what was behind that vault door. Zenrot moved to get a closer look. The vault was circle in shape, and was about ten feet tall. It looked like it only opened with a combination number. Zenrot punched the vault many times trying to bust it open, but the vault was still intact. He hadn't left even a single dent in it.

"Don't even bother," Astred advised, getting closer to the vault and knocking on it a couple of times. "This thing is made with pure steel and reinforced concrete, among other elements. It will take high explosives to break it down."

"Why not break the walls around it until we can reach inside?" Freddy suggested.

"This vault is designed with concrete steel in all four walls on the inside. Assuming Sentry Run made this vault to resist mutant abilities… Only way to destroy it would be with the power of a nuke or two. If we do that, we destroy what's inside as well."

"And that's why we're opening this thing," Zenrot said, glancing at Astred. "Can you hack the combination of this vault to get us inside?"

"I can try, but it may take a couple of minutes."

"Do it," Zenrot ordered. Astred moves close to the passcode machine, searching through his backpack and finds a device. He connected a gadget to the passcode machine, its display cycling through different random sets of numbers; it was trying different combinations to open the vault.

"I don't know why… but I have a bad feeling about this," Freddy said anxiously.

"Same here, we should probably head on our way and finish the mission. Who knows what other surprises we may face?"

Zenrot turned to Keishla and Freddy. "Right now, we must defend Astred while he works on the vault. Soon we see what's inside, and we'll be on our way. Remember, Arashi wants anything useful we can find—"

Keishla rushed angrily toward Zenrot and confront him.

"Fuck Arashi! We should worry about ourselves! We're the only bastards who got sent on this mission. How are they going to know?"

Zenrot took a few steps backwards to create some space from Keishla. "They may not see what we do, but aren't you forgetting why we're here? To be the—"

"The best mutants for humanity. We are the examples, blah, blah… yeah, I get that crap," Keishla mocked as she walked back to Freddy. "I just feel that there is something they aren't telling us." She turns herself around, "Like you, of course."

"Ok, you're not making sense." Zenrot sounded irritated. "The hell are you trying to say?"

"The way you use that special gun of yours. You wiped the robots out like nothing back in the hallway. What other abilities can you use which we don't know about?"

"I figured that out in the moment. And I still feel a bit drained from that attack." He slowly walked closer to Keishla, trying to keep things balanced before an unnecessary fight occurred. "Besides, I can say the same for you. I didn't know you knew how to use a sword before today. You never once told me about it back in base. Honestly, I still don't know what I'm capable of. So don't start with the trust issues now."

"Don't you play smart with me, Zenrot."

"Keishla, we all have grown stronger step by step." Freddy joined the conversation with his hands in the air, miming surrender. "Everyone always learns new things. So don't overreact to *that*."

"*Mph!* Speaking of trust… why did Arashi ask for your presence only a few days back?"

"…I can't say."

"Uh, why not?"

"It's… complicated."

"If you're worried about us saying something, we won't tell on you." Keishla shifted her gaze to Zenrot. "I'll make sure of that." Zenrot was amazed that, after all the years working together, she still disbelieved him and he walked away. "Come on, you can tell us." Before Freddy could speak, the vault made a noise.

Astred had managed to open it. Keishla believed it was a mistake, there was a reason why the vault was too strong for anyone to break into. She insist to leave it alone. Zenrot told Keishla to stop overthinking, and Freddy was surprised how both were still arguing. *These two are like little kids fighting,* he thought.

Meanwhile, Astred watched how the vault slowly opened. When it was completely open, Astred took out a flashlight and looked around. Everyone was surprised. There was nothing inside the vault.

Wondering why they had bothered making a strong security room if there was nothing to secure, Astred believed the people of Sentry Run had taken all important data inside the vault. However, to Zenrot, that didn't make sense. Arashi had told them everyone was killed inside the building, including the workers.

Whatever happened inside the headquarters, whoever attacked, hadn't let anyone evacuate. Taking personal stuff from the vault would have taken a lot of time they didn't had. Something wasn't right.

"I don't know about you guys, but I agree with Keishla on one thing," Zenrot said, "we are missing some intel here. Something that Arashi may not have mentioned back at base." He sounded confused.

"Agreed," Astred said as he walked inside the vault. "Let's just get this mission done and look for more information about it later. I have a feeling that Arashi is up to something else."

Zenrot grew concerned at that statement. "What do you mean?" he asked.

Astred turned around, looking at his team. "In my hypothesis, it could be that—"

"Astred, look out!" Keishla shouted. Astred dropped into a crouch as he turned around, his arm flowing with nanomachines as he threw his fist. It knocked an enemy robot away from him and against the wall. More robots appeared from the shadows.

"Frederick! Light up this room!" Astred shouted.

Freddy threw flames in the air to see inside the vault. It had changed; it wasn't empty anymore. Spartans waited inside, along with a new type of robot designed with hoods, looking like assassins. There was a word painted in white on the right side of their hood, "Nocturne." They were smaller than a Golem or a Spartan, but moved fast and sneakily. Zenrot looked around inside the vault; There were more robots than anyone could count: it was a trap.

The Nocturnes' arms shaped into spears. All of them ready to attack Astred. One Nocturne got ahead and tried to stab his chest, but he caught the spear and swung the robot into its allies. Another Nocturne, tried with a blade, swinging at Astred to slice him into pieces. His body changed into steel and the Nocturne's attacks bounced harmlessly off. Astred punched the Nocturne, blowing it back to crash into the other robots.

Unfortunately, more enemies kept coming. Astred was outnumbered.

"Hold on! We're on our way!" Zenrot screamed as he, Keishla, and Freddy ran to Astred. Spartans flooded the space to stop them, however, with their spears aiming at Zenrot and the others. Zenrot used his gun to shoot an energy bullet and Freddy raised his hand to release fire, each hitting the Spartans with everything they had. Their shields held together despite the combined attack, and the robots got closer and closer, ready to stab the three of them.

Luckily, Astred threw a Nocturne into the Spartans from the back. Keishla took the opportunity to cut them down. "Are you guys all right?"

"We're fine, thanks to you!" Zenrot answered back.

"Good, let's get out of here while we still—AGH!"

"ASTRED!" Zenrot and Keishla shouted.

Astred looked down to his stomach where a spear had managed to stab him from the back, despite the steel of his skin. The Nocturne removed the spear and Astred collapsed to his knees. As he looked at the Nocturne's spear, a strange goo, silver in color, was coming out of the weapon. Whatever it was, it seemed like it was the liquid that had bypassed Astred's steel.

"The Nocturnes..." Astred said weakly, "Sentry Run gave them weapons and materials to use against our weaknesses..." A Nocturne jumped high and threw itself, spear-first, to stab Astred from above. He moved aside and grabbed the spear with one hand, smashing the robot while removing the weapon from its body. He threw it at other Nocturnes farther away, piercing five of them as the spear rocketed towards the wall at the far end of the room. Astred's hand was burning. The strange goo had dripped from the spear before he threw it, coating his hand and melting away his steel.

"Zenrot, Keishla, Frederick!" Astred screamed as they kept fighting more Spartans. "The Nocturnes have an unidentified weapon that can burn deeply into the strongest concrete! Use ranged attack if you must—AGH!"

"ASTRED!" Zenrot screamed his name loudly. Another Nocturne had stabbed him with a blade from the back. His steel was slowly disappearing; most of his flesh had returned to normal at this point. Zenrot ran to help Astred, but he got knocked away by a Spartan's shield. He drew and aimed at the Nocturne attacking Astred and shot at its head, destroying the robot completely. He rolled away to dodge the Spartan's spear, giving an opening for Frederick to slice its head off with his scythe.

Zenrot turned to look at Astred. He was running away from the Nocturnes. He grabbed a Spartan's body with both hands and threw it at the Nocturnes, taking several more of them down at the same time. Rather than continuing toward the rest of the team, though, Astred fell to the ground, completely still and with the blade in his back.

"Go!" Freddy shouted, "Help Astred! Keishla and I will handle these metalheads!"

Zenrot nodded and dashed to Astred's side. He slid in on his knees, raising Astred with both hands.

"Astred!" Zenrot sounded agitated. "Come on, we gotta get out of here!" Zenrot put Astred's arm over his shoulder, and drag him to get outside the vault. "Come on! We got this—"

"Dark Boy, look out!" Keishla warned him. All the Nocturnes were heading toward Zenrot and Astred. Six of them were moving in close, taking advantage of the fact that he was off guard. Zenrot couldn't let go of Astred, so his first instinct was to take out his gun and shoot the robots down. but before he could act, he was pulled into a hug by Astred, covering him from the attack. His back was exposed to the Nocturnes, skin turning into silver.

"AGHHHHHHHHHH!"

"ASTRED!" Zenrot shouts in pain as he watched Astred's face, gritting his teeth. Astred turned around and he removed some of the blade left in his back, throwing it heavily at the first Nocturne he saw ahead. He hit it in the chest and with a single fist of steel blow it away.

Astred was falling again, but Zenrot grabbed him in time before he fell to the ground.

"Astred!" Keishla shouted furiously. Heartbroken, she desperately threw herself into fighting all the Nocturnes. She used her sword to slice them into pieces. The Nocturnes were easy to break, but they were also as fast as Keishla. There were too many to handle by herself. A Nocturne was about to stab her from behind while she was fighting. She heard the noise of a blade and quickly looked back; Freddy had saved her, surrounding the robots with fire. Keishla and Freddy were fighting the Nocturnes, but the Spartans were arriving as reinforcements.

Zenrot took the opportunity to take Astred away from the vault. He laid Astred on the floor, looking for any solution to heal him, but Astred had many wounds on his body. He was bleeding tremendously from all the stabs and burns left by the strange goo.

"Please hang in there, Astred!" Zenrot begged, breathing unevenly and agitated as his heartbeat climbed. He was looking for something—anything!—at this point to save Astred's life.

Astred coughed, trying to speak. "Listen… you must continue the mission… save yourselves while you still can—"

"NO! I won't let you die! This is all my fault. We should have left when we had the chance…" Zenrot spoke with blame.

Astred grabbed his shirt weakly. "It's ok… you didn't know." He pulled Zenrot a bit closer, trying to speak as softly as he could. "Listen closely, Zenrot." He raised his other hand, pressing something into his friend's palm. "This is an electronic device you must put into the computers of floor twenty-five, you must get the intel and eliminate Project V…" He coughed heavier as the pain increased.

Zenrot was drowning in tears as he saw how Astred struggled to speak.

"Be careful with Arashi… There is something strange

happening." Astred looked directly into Zenrot's eyes. Miraculously enough, he had a smile on his face. "No matter what happens, stay with Keishla … you two share the same pain and courage, please take care of each other. Zenrot… my partner…" His grip failed, the hand fell to the floor and Zenrot couldn't find his pulse.

Astred was gone.

After his last words, Zenrot wiped his tears with his arm, trying to get himself together. He rejoined Keishla and Freddy in the fight.

"Where's Astred?" Keishla asked, swinging her sword in a wide arc through a Spartan; she cut it in half. "Zenrot! Where is Astred?"

"He's gone!" Zenrot yelled, blocking a Nocturne's attack with his sword. Zenrot pushed the robot away and blew it up with an energy shot. "We must continue our mission!"

"We are not leaving Astred!" Keishla dodged another Spartan's attack and stabbed it through the head with a dagger, which then floated obediently back to her. "We can still help—"

"HE'S GONE!" Zenrot screamed, firing at a Spartan after Spartan. "There's no turning back!"

"This is your fault! We should've stuck with the original plan!"

"Can we please focus?" Freddy shouted louder to make them concentrate on fighting. He whirled his scythe around, slicing the Nocturnes near him. When he had a chance to speak, he turned around and yelled, "Zenrot! What are your orders?"

"Kill all these bastards!" Zenrot rushed forward, slashing a

Spartan with his sword while firing his revolver at other robots, to make them overload and explode.

"Best idea you've had so far!" Keishla followed. She ran as fast as she could, releasing energy into her sword and rapidly slashing every visible weak point the Spartans and Nocturnes had. Anywhere that thick metal wasn't covering their bodies took a blow from her blade. Everyone was fighting at the same time, but there was no end to the swarm of Spartans and Nocturnes. Zenrot holstered his gun, switching the grip on his sword to both hands and, with all his strength, slicing through the Spartans one by one. When he turned around, a Nocturne was in the air and kick him right in the face. The blow knocked him away, rolling across the floor.

"Zenrot!" Freddy shouted. He pushed away a Spartan that was clashing its spear against Freddy's scythe and, realizing the Nocturne was about to stab Zenrot with a strange dagger, he quickly charged the blade of his scythe. He threw a slash of fire, slicing the Nocturne that made it melt.

When Freddy turned back around to fight, a Spartan was already in front of him. It struck him with a shield charge, right in the chest. He bounced all the way to Zenrot who grabbed Freddy out of the air. They fell to the ground together as the Spartan charged closer, trying to stab them with his spear. Zenrot took his gun out of the holster and charged enough energy to shoot. An energy beam passed through the Spartan's chest; it fell, crashing heavily to the floor.

Keishla saw more Spartans approaching them. She ran with her daggers floating in the air, throwing them at the necks of several Spartans, where there was a weak spot from their metal armor. While running, Nocturnes showed up, matching her speed. One attack with the dagger on its hand. Bringing her daggers with her telekinesis, Keishla slashed the arm then slid herself to the floor. While the Nocturnes kept running, she sliced their legs with one swing of her sword.

When she stood back up, another Nocturne had already appeared at her right side. It jumped to kick Keishla. The Nocturne was about to hit her when Keishla raised her arm to protect herself, and by making a bad move, the Nocturne hit her arm hard enough with its metal leg to push her entire body back. Keishla screamed in pain, but it didn't stop her from retaliating. All her daggers aimed at that Nocturne and, propelled by her telekinesis, they all rocketed forward. Some bounced away because of the metal reinforcement, but others managed to penetrate the robot. While it was stunned, Keishla stretched her right arm, quickly shaking it to try and mitigate the pain. She grabbed her sword and slashed the Nocturne from different angles until it finally was shattered into pieces. Keishla ran straight to Zenrot and Freddy, crouching to take a breather beside them. Another enemy tried to ambush her, but Zenrot jumped over Keishla, kicked the Nocturne far away, then shot it in midair.

"I got you!" Zenrot yelled, agitated. "Stand up! We aren't done yet."

"They just keep coming!" Keishla shouted, taking her feet to fight again.

Reinforcements kept coming and it was clear there were

too many to handle. Freddy came up with an idea to clear the battlefield.

"Guys, I have a plan! But it will cost a *lot* of my energy. Both of you need to get to cover!"

"To hell with that! We are not leaving you with these techno bots!" Keishla said furiously, making it clear there was no way she'd risk losing another team member.

"We don't have many choices right now! If we keep doing this, we all are going to die here! I'll be fine! Just cover my back if anything goes wrong… now go!"

Zenrot got the message, nodded, then yelled for Keishla to take cover away from the vault. When they got outside his estimated danger radius, Freddy started charging an immense amount of energy in his hand. He was building up a giant fire blast to wipe out everyone on the battlefield. All the robots were rushing towards Freddy to stop his attack.

"HOPE YOU ALL ROT IN HELL!" he screamed. The robots were close from hitting Freddy, but he released the energy, blasting apart the entire room and everything inside it. Fire spread to every corner, shattering the robots into ashes. The building shook. Zenrot and Keishla could feel the heat but were far enough away to be safe from the blast.

The heat felt less intense, so Zenrot slowly made his way to see inside the vault. The room had completely burned away, but the fire was starting to fade. Freddy had destroyed them all. Slowly turning around, he noticed Zenrot was watching.

"Heh… told you I had a plan…" Freddy closed his eyes, falling to the floor. Zenrot ran towards Freddy, grabbing him before he touched the ground and putting two fingers on Freddy's neck to check if there's any pulse. He was still breathing. That was a relief. Zenrot gently lifted Freddy, carrying him on his back out of the vault.

As Zenrot got out, he found Keishla close to Astred's body, in tears, mourning his death. He couldn't believe Astred was really gone. Almost more unsettling, it was the first time Zenrot had seen Keishla emotional like that. Who could blame her? Like she had said before, Astred was like a father to her.

"Keishla," Zenrot said gently, "I know it's hard, but we must keep going. The sooner we finish, the faster we can get the hell out of here. I need you strong. Please…" Keishla tried to hold herself together. She brushed away her tears and moved to help Zenrot with Freddy. She provided cover while they slowly made their way to the next floor. Keishla demanded they call for extraction for Freddy and for Art Gun to send reinforcements. She refused to lose another member of the MSF. On the next floor, Keishla carefully scouted the hallway, finding no enemies. She suggested laying Freddy down and calling Art Gun. Gently letting go of Freddy, Zenrot searched his pocket for his communicator, then put it into his ear, trying to communicate.

"Zenrot to Arashi, do you copy? Over."

"Arashi here, what's your status?"

"Not good, we need an extraction for Frederick Crossvelt. He needs medical attention as soon as possible. We also request reinforcements to help us against all enemy robots in this building. This place is too dangerous for us to manage on our own!"

"Have you completed the mission?

"No, sir! That's why we require immediate assistance."

"I'm afraid I must deny your request. The mission must be completed. We can't risk any more troops."

"Sir! Astred has been neutralized! Freddy is unconscious! Keishla and I can hardly stand for ourselves in these conditions. We need help!"

"I'm sorry Zenrot, but my orders are clear: complete the mission whatever the cost. I will send someone for extraction when it's finished. Right now, your team is on your own... out." After their discussion, Arashi hung up. Zenrot couldn't believe he had turned them down. They were close to reaching their destination, yet so far from achieving their goals. Freddy was barely in any condition to stand. Keishla looked like she could still fight, but the question was for how long. She looked exhausted.

Zenrot refused to go down that easily, though, and knew Keishla felt the same. Zenrot wondered if that was what Astred meant by staying together; that he'd known they were too stubborn to quit. Perhaps he had known Arashi would turn them down. If that was true, it spawned several other questions. Arashi had worked hard to build this team and invested a lot of resources into their success. Why simply let it go to waste? Too many theories were competing for attention within Zenrot's mind.

Keishla noticed he was spaced out from the look on his face, and that it was obvious there wasn't any good news.

"What is it?" she asked.

Zenrot shook his head. "I'm afraid… we are on our own."

"The hell you mean?"

"That we must complete our task ourselves. One way or another."

CHAPTER
SIX

"Fucking assholes!" Keishla screamed in anger as they reached floor nineteen. Keishla is carrying Freddy while Zenrot was on guard in case of an ambush. "When we get back to Art Gun, I promise you I will grab Arashi by the goatee and use his head as practice shot!"

"Save that rage for the enemies," Zenrot suggested as he crept ahead with his hand on the hilt of his sword. "We need to finish the mission if we want to get out of here."

"Still… I can't believe they'll just leave us like this."

"We will seek answers," Zenrot said as he swept the next hallway with his revolver, keeping ahold of the grip of the sword with his other hand. "The more I think about it, the more I remember what Astred was about to say before he—" Zenrot paused, not finishing the sentence. He hoped he hadn't triggered Keishla's grief. "I think he knew something. Just hope we find out why."

Looking at a distance, Zenrot scanned the next room. Electric spikes spread across it. He scouted ahead to secure the area, but when Zenrot reached the room, he only saw broken robots on the floor.

"It's clear," he informed Keishla. She entered the room with Freddy on her back.

Keishla gently put him on the floor, sitting Freddy against a wall. She took a good look at the room. There were plenty of destroyed Golems and Spartans. The place was a mess. One thing was for certain, it hadn't been either Zenrot or Keishla. Someone else did this. In the distance they saw five big machines. Each was shaped like a capsule, but with a glass portion on the front. Zenrot and Keishla walked close to examine them. The first three of them were untouched, filled with water and another substance inside—something unknown that looked like a semisolid goo. The fourth capsule had shattered crystal, and the fifth capsule was open to the room; the glass portion was raised up. Under the capsule machines, there was a sign. One that's opened: *Project V.* It had also a description under the name: *An experiment that copies the opponents' abilities and duplicates any kind of energy.* They were close to their target.

Zenrot and Keishla continued exploring the room. The remains of soldiers from Art Gun were in the room. Corpses gathered on top of one another. Keishla wanted to vomit from the horrible smell. Some bodies looked like they had been there for a long time. Zenrot took a closer look to identify the bodies. He saw the yellow ranked team… first Bravo, then Charlie, and finally Delta.

"It can't be…" he said as he looked at their uniforms. He was shocked to see familiar faces. Only now they were less familiar, all having that strange silver goo beneath their skin and with other portions of their flesh chewed or blown away. "This was Brandolf's team." Zenrot couldn't see Brandolf's body, but he was certain Brandolf wasn't alive. They'd disappeared for years. Keishla noticed the silver goo in and on their bodies; the same one material that was inside the capsule machines.

"This Project V," Keishla said, frightened, "what kind of weapon is it exactly?"

"Honestly… I don't know."

They both had many questions about the threat Project V posed. Because of the way Arashi had described it, the weapon sounded like a gun anyone could handle. Judging from the giant capsules, seems like it handled itself; *someone* had been created inside.

Keishla walked back to the first capsule, grabbing a dagger from her backpack, stabbing the crystal and the glass shattered. The water inside flooded out, displacing the strange goo onto the floor as well. Noticing it was moving, Keishla raised another dagger and stabbed the goo. It made a noise that sounded almost like a scream. Keishla made sure that whatever it was didn't finish developing. Her gaze moved to Zenrot.

"We can't let any of these things be seen by Art Gun." Keishla moved to the second capsule and did the same as the first one. "After your conversation with Arashi, it's safe to say we can't trust them with this information. These are prodigies that have a connection with Project V. We can't let this fall into the wrong hands."

Zenrot was anxious that she wanted to destroy everything, feeling that this was valuable information. But he also acknowledged that Keishla was right; Arashi had turned him down for extraction and refused to send reinforcements. It was hard to trust his intuition.

After Zenrot's decision back in the vault, his confidence was shaken. He didn't want to make a mistake like that again. Zenrot nodded, agreeing to Keishla's terms, and went to destroy the third capsule. He took out his gun and shot the information plates as well, making sure there wasn't any evidence left.

A growl interrupted Zenrot's thought. Both mutants momentarily panicked. The sound seemed to come from the twentieth floor. Zenrot immediately ordered Keishla to grab Freddy and stay behind. They cautiously proceeded to the main stairs and up to the next floor.

When Zenrot and Keishla reached floor twenty, everything was dark. There were more corpses on the ground; some with the uniform of Art Gun and others wearing the uniform of Sentry Run. Zenrot warned Keishla to keep her distance and moved ahead. The room was very quiet. He could only hear their footsteps as they walked inside. The main stairs ended on that floor, and the elevator to go up was on lockdown. From the other side of the room, there was a visible light flashing: a sign that indicated the stairs to floor twenty-one.

"I'll go check if it's clear to engage," Zenrot said quietly, slowly walking forward to keep an eye on everything. He moved in the position he'd adopted throughout most of the mission: with his revolver in one hand, holding the handle of his sword with the other.

"Are you nuts? You don't know what we're dealing with."

"We need to keep going, otherwise we'll be stuck here. We don't have much choice." Zenrot stopped, searching in his pockets. He took out the device Astred gave him. Zenrot turned to show it to Keishla. "If I don't make it, I want you to take this and install it onto their main computer and download every piece of information you can." Zenrot put it in her pocket since she was carrying Freddy. "Once you do that, call for an extraction from the top of this building and take Freddy with you." Zenrot turned and moved on ahead.

"You're not going to stay here, you hear me? We'll finish this together."

Zenrot shook his head. "It's my fault we're in this situation. I'm going to make this right." He was ashamed because he believed it was his fault for Astred's death.

"By killing yourself?" Keishla said angrily. "Don't be stupid! If anyone will kill you it'll be me beating the shit out of you. We're all getting out of here, period!"

Zenrot held out a hand and shut her up. He heard something approaching slowly, taking heavy steps. Each one sounded like an engine getting louder. Keishla saw something strange appear behind Zenrot.

"Behind you!" Keishla shouted in panicked. Zenrot looked back and took out his sword. Her warning had been enough to get him moving; the sword was in the right place to block the surprise attack. Zenrot jumped away and the strange enemy rushed to attack. Reacting quickly, Zenrot stood firmly and made a single kick directly to the enemy's face, forcing him away. The strange assailant landed on the ground but stood back up like it was nothing. Zenrot took a closer look. The attacker was someone with a humanoid shape, but with a body that was entirely white and silver. It had no face; there was only a symbol glowing in red in the shape of the letter "V" where the face should have been.

"I think we found our target," Zenrot said, gasping. Project V's sharp blades were softening and changing into regular hands. "It looks like it's a shapeshifter." The Project stood still for a moment, seeming to stare at Zenrot despite its lack of a face. A red dot projected from the symbol scanned Zenrot up and down. The project growled and formed his hand like Zenrot's revolver, then rapidly began to charge a massive energy bullet. Zenrot jumped away and a tremendous energy shot went past, hit a wall, and blasted it apart. When Zenrot looked at the wall, the energy blast had passed through everything in the way. He could see clearly outside of the building.

"Zenrot, look out!" Keishla yelled. Zenrot looked back to the front. Project V was standing close with his blade. He attacked, but Zenrot dodged by moving his body back. The blade passed in front of Zenrot's chest, and he tried to counterattack. He grabbed his sword with both hands, swinging it quickly from every direction.

Project V dodged every attack, bending his whole body away from the sword. He then pressed an opportunity, attacking with his hand-as-a-sword against Zenrot. Their blades clashed against one another. Zenrot noticed Project V's combat skill, the same way Ryan had taught him how to fight with a sword. He copied every technique. Project V attacked from above with his blade, but Zenrot blocked the attack with his sword. Project V excelled in both speed and strength.

Keishla noticed Zenrot was struggling and looked around to find a safe spot for Freddy so she could join the fight. Looking at the room they were in, she could understand why it had ambushed them there: it was practically a giant arena, and there wasn't any safe place to hide.

Zenrot pushed Project V away, creating an opening. He took out his revolver with one hand, aiming it at Project V's chest and blowing him away. The experiment impacted against another wall.

Zenrot gazed back and noticed Keishla's intention.

"Don't even bother!" Zenrot screamed. "Take the device I gave you and head to Sentry Run's main computer! I got this one." Project V had splashed silver goo all over the floor. It was slowly moving towards, completely reforming his body.

"Are you crazy?" Keishla shouted. "There is no way I'll leave you with that slimeball!" She moved to the nearest wall to lay Freddy against it. Project V had almost completed his reformation, but Zenrot took another shot with his revolver and exploded Project V into pieces again. This time, the goo moved faster. "Fuck that! I'm helping you—"

"STOP!" Zenrot screamed without hesitation. He looked at her with his eyes wide open. "If you help, Project V will adapt to your abilities and copy them as well. If that happens, it'll be impossible to kill this thing! Go get the intel and finish this mission, I'll catch up to you."

"FUCK NO! You are NOT going to stay alone with this giant slimeball!"

"I GAVE YOU AN ORDER! Get the hell out of here and take Freddy with you! I will hold him off!" Zenrot screamed angrily so Keishla would get the message. He felt guilty for yelling that way, but it was the only way she'd listen. Keishla didn't agree with Zenrot's plan, but Freddy was still unconscious. He would be exposed if Keishla decided to fight.

Following Zenrot's orders, Keishla took Freddy and headed to the emergency stairs. Project V finished completely repairing himself and saw Keishla running away. He sprinted to attack, but Zenrot got in the way and slashed him with the sword, cutting his right arm. When the arms reached the floor, they turned into a blob of liquid silver which attached to his leg and flowed up toward the stomach. From there, it moved all the way back to form his arm again. Zenrot was amazed for such a difficult opponent—amazed and afraid. His eyes were wide open in fear as he looked back to see if Keishla went to the next level.

On the emergency stairs, she stopped and turned around to look directly at Zenrot.

"You better come back in one piece, you hear me? Don't make me get your sorry ass later." Keishla finally left onto the next floor. Zenrot stayed alone with Project V. With his sword in hand, he approached his opponent.

Project V was standing still, contorting his body in the toughest way possible to avoid being hit. He scanned Zenrot, analyzing his skills yet again. He used the exact same moves against Zenrot while reforming his hands into sharp blades.

Project V engaged, swinging his blades so fast he cut Zenrot's left side of his arm, then his upper chest, his right leg—cuts opened across almost every part of Zenrot's body. Out of frustration, he used his revolver and fired many small shots as he backed away from Project V. When smoke started coming out and, seeing no immediate attack from the enemy, Zenrot kneeled to rest a few seconds and recover a bit of energy. He looked warily at Project V.

Zenrot considered theories about what could have happened in the building with Project V roaming around. *The soldiers never made it out because this thing got released and killed everyone in the building. Yet robots are still wandering around, attacking intruders. Which means it's designed to kill actual living things: mutants or humans,* he thought. Project V jumped high into the air, attempting to come down on Zenrot with a sharp blade on his hand. He tried to stab Zenrot from above, but he rolled out of his way, dodging the attack. *Not only that... he copies any of my attacks and makes weapons with his own body,* Zenrot stated.

Project V turned his blade into liquid, unsticking himself from the floor. The liquid turned back into an arm. *Yet his energy is mixed with many things... which may have to do with the mutants Sentry Run took hostage to create this weapon. I must destroy it before Project V gets stronger and tries something new, otherwise I'm done for!* Zenrot stated. He stood up, dark energy pouring from his hands and flowing over his sword. He pointed his gun at Project V and shot him with a blast of energy. Project V dodged the energy blast, but Zenrot had planned for that and moved in fast enough to be able to reach him before

Project V shifted his attention from dodging the shot.

With his sword in a one-handed grip, Zenrot started attacking from different angles, slashing the white and silver creature into pieces which fell, unceremoniously, to the floor. Zenrot jumped back away from Project V.

"Did I get him?" he asked himself, surprised. His budding optimism sank, however, when Zenrot heard a growl. Project V's pieces were automatically putting him back together. He reassembled into his original form once again, and Zenrot couldn't be more frustrated. No matter what attack he used, Project V still reformed itself back. Its body didn't show evidence that a single scratch had been inflicted. Project V quickly scanned Zenrot, releasing a ball of energy and throwing it at him. Zenrot jumped back and away from the energy, but when it touched the floor there was an explosion that caused the room to shake.

Zenrot was shocked at how quickly Project V adapted to both his abilities and energy. He sprinted at maximum speed toward Zenrot and started attacking with his hands already formed into blades. Zenrot parried at the same speed with his sword. The fight was getting more difficult, and he knew he needed to find a way to put Project V down that the enemy couldn't stand back up from.

Well, this is going to be tough, Zenrot thought.

CHAPTER
SEVEN

Keishla carried Freddy all the way to floor twenty-five. It was a long road going up the stairs with all that weight. Luckily, there weren't any enemies along the way.

"Damn it Freddy, I hope you wake up sometime soon." She searched her surroundings for the objective. Keishla saw something ahead of them. Things were crawling around, leaving traces of silver goo while they moved. They looked like tiny humans unfinished, only formed from head to waist, and were almost the same material as Project V. Keishla took a step back away from the enemy, accidentally stepping on a piece of broken glass. All the creatures looked to where the noise came from and noticed Keishla's presence. They had no facial expression or symbol on them. They started crawling closer using their hands, moving as a pack. The swarm was on its way to attack Keishla.

"Ew! What the hell am I supposed to call you guys? Project Clambers?" Keishla quickly looked around for a place to hide Freddy so she could defend herself, but there was none.

Fortunately, Freddy started to wake up. There was struggle in his voice, though. Freddy was still exhausted for using most of his energy. He wouldn't be able to help Keishla on the battlefield.

"Put me… on the ground… Go," Freddy said quietly through gritted teeth. Keishla gently put him down against the wall. Hearing the Clambers getting closer, Keishla released all her daggers from her backpack. She started slashing them one by one, then ran straight to attack with her sword. She focused energy through the blade to make better impacts and slash them into pieces. Silver goo spilled all over the place. After finishing them all, Keishla walked back to Freddy but then she heard something unsettling.

She looked over her shoulder, noticing that the Clambers were slowly reforming back to their original shapes. Keishla tried to eliminate them once again. Some turned into complete liquid. Finally thought she had found a way to kill them, then noticed they were melting the ground… then transforming back into their form.

"Oh, come on! How do I kill these things?"

"You don't…" Keishla gasped, turning for a quick look at Freddy. He was finally awake.

"You sound like you're getting better." She crouched closer to him. Can you fight?" She asked.

Freddy was still sitting on the ground, laying with his back against the wall. He slowly raised his hand. He tried to release fire, but only sparks of heat come out. "I can't," he said softly. "Still feel drained from all that energy. Need a few minutes to recover."

"God, you're a sissy." Keishla looked back again, returning all her daggers to her backpack. "Can you walk?"

"Yeah."

"Good. You find a place to hide. I'll make these guys follow me and lose them on my way to the twenty-fifth floor. Then I'll find the main computer and download every crappy piece of intel I can get. I'll contact you when it's done." Keishla stood up, sprinting as fast as she could to pass through the Clambers. She slashed a few as she ran away.

"Hey, germ freaks! Catch me if you can!" She wasn't sure if they could understand her, but she taunted them as she ran away. Heading to the emergency stairs, the Clambers were crawling too fast. Luckily, as she climbed the stairs the Clambers bumped into one another since there were so many of them. She used her energy to move at maximum speed until, finally, she reached floor twenty-five. At the end of the room there was a giant gate with the doors shut and Keishla saw a switch button. She sprinted quickly to push it.

"ACCESSING THE MAIN LAB. PLEASE STAND BY," an intercom spoke. The gates were opening slowly. While waiting to get inside, Keishla heard the Clambers arriving. She turned, releasing her telekinetic daggers and sending them to attack. She cuts them down piece by piece, preventing them from getting closer. The gate finally opened behind her.

Keishla quickly slipped into the room and saw a button labeled "LOCKDOWN." Keishla smashed it with her fist, and the room instantly locked with a pair of stronger doors. She could hear the Clambers from the other side.

"I hope Freddy finds another way. Not getting my ass melted by some half boogers!" Keishla turned around, looking at a giant lab with different weapons she had never seen before. There were different unfinished robots, custom guns, and blueprints everywhere. Far in the distance, there were bodies with their chests opened and heads left in different states. Keishla couldn't hold it and went to a corner to vomit. "God!" She coughed as she cleans her mouth. "Those were mutants that were taken hostage. What the hell were these guys doing?" Trying to focus on the mission, Keishla walked around the room and found the giant computer with all the cables behind it. It looked to be connected to the whole building. "Think I found our objective."

Keishla got close to the computer and turned it on. The screens were asking for a password to access the computer. Keishla took the device out from her pocket.

"Well, do your thing, Astred." She inserted the device that looked like a personalized floppy disk to the computer, and it automatically put in a password, accessed the computer, and started downloading all the intel. Keishla saw information across the monitor; blueprints, coordinates of invasions, mutant analyses… everything data about Sentry Run.

While Keishla waited for everything to download, she moved to examine the weapons and equipment attached on one wall, searching if there was anything useful for battle. Keishla picked two in the shape of waves, some metal wires, and a small staff. She also saw a piece of armor: a pauldron. Under the pauldron there was a small needle that could flip down. She found it weird, but looked useful to her. Tucking a few pauldrons and the other materials into her backpack, Keishla returned to check the status of the computer. It was about to finish. Watching the last pieces of information flit across the screen, she noticed something strange.

Keishla saw details about Zenrot, Freddy, Astred, and herself on the monitor. It appeared that Sentry Run had studied them from a video record that was transmitted back from sensors in a robot's head. Before she could read anything in the report, the download finished, and the computer shut down.

"WARNING, INTRUDERS DETECTED IN THE MAIN LAB. INITIATE HEADQUARTERS SELF-DESTRUCT IN TEN MINUTES," an alarm sounded all over the building.

"That's not a good sign." Keishla grabbed the device, looking for a way out. The main door was shut, and the Clambers were still on the other side. She looked around and saw a pack of weapons laying on a store box. Keishla ran to it, searching for explosives. There was a wide selection inside, and she found herself a few blocks of C4. She looked up at the ceiling. *That's my way out.* Keishla focused her energy aura at her feet, crouched, and jumped as high as she could. She stuck the C4 to the ceiling and, finding cover, pulled the trigger.

BOOM. The ceiling crumbled down, making her way out. She leapt again to floor twenty-six, then rushed her way toward the roof. "This is Keishla, do you read me? Over." Keishla tried to contact Arashi as she ran.

"This is Arashi here, what's your status?"

"Mission accomplished, got the intel you needed, and Dark Boy is eliminating Project V. We request immediate extraction at the top of this damn building! This place will explode in less than ten minutes!"

"Copy that, I'll inform the standby pilot to fly to the top of the building. Make sure everyone is there on time, we can't risk staying too long, out." Arashi signed off as Keishla found another emergency door. She continued climbing the stairs all the way to the roof.

"Dark Boy, Freddy! Keishla reporting in… This building is about to explode in less than ten minutes. I got the intel and I'm on my way to the extraction point. The helicopter is coming for us at the top of the building. Whatever you're doing, make it fast—they won't wait for us for too long."

"Wait, you left Freddy behind?" Zenrot shouted through their communicator. Keishla could hear the fighting in the background.

"It's all right, I told her to keep on with the mission. I'll be on my way to the roof, how's everything with you, Zenrot?" The way Freddy was speaking was better than before.

"Still with Project V, AGH! This thing is tougher than I thought it would be!" Keishla could hear the clash between his sword and the blades of Project V.

"Listen here, Dark Boy, you better get over here and save yourself. Leave Project V behind and let it blow up with this building."

"As much as I love that plan," gunshots were heard in the background, *"this thing can regenerate. Pretty sure it will survive the explosion, so you two need to get away. I'll make sure this bastard doesn't go anywhere."*

Keishla started yelling at the mic. "You do whatever it takes to destroy Project V, but don't you dare stay down there and die! I will go there and drag you all the way to the roof if I must. I won't lose another teammate, you hear me? Now kill that giant slimeball already and come up here! OUT!"

"Geez. You better make it, mini-chief, I'm almost there. Good luck. Out."

***

Zenrot was chuckling because, despite how she had treated him, Keishla still cared. He was on his knees with his sword in his left hand and his gun in the right. His forehead was bleeding and most of his was body injured. Project V was still standing, with barely any injuries. Zenrot slowly climbed to his feet and dashed to attack with his sword. No matter how many times he tried, Project V kept dodging all the incoming attacks. When Project V had an opportunity, it charged a small portion of energy from his hand and hit Zenrot with a single blow. It pushed him away until Zenrot collided with the wall, bouncing to the ground.

Struggling to stand up, Zenrot spit blood from his mouth, thinking of a way to finish the battle. *Physical attacks won't work. Neither does small amounts of energy from my abilities. Every movement I make, he's two steps ahead of me... guess I have no choice,* he thought. Zenrot adjusted his grip on the revolver, charging it with all the energy accumulated from his body.

Project V renewed its attack on Zenrot, but he focused on dodging while charging his gun. He was almost finished. Project

93

V turned his fingers into claws and stabbed him—one hand stabbed into Zenrot's arm holding the sword, while the other pierced his stomach. Project V started releasing silver liquid inside of Zenrot, burning him from inside his own body.

Zenrot screamed in pain and headbutt Project V as a quick reaction. He was forced to release Zenrot, but as Project V backed away, he sliced Zenrot's chest with the tip of his claws. Zenrot threw himself back, lifting his revolver and pointing it at Project V.

"This is the part when you go to hell!" Zenrot shot him with an immense energy burst. The blast hit Project V, going all the way outside of the building.

Zenrot collapsed to the ground in exhaustion.

Watching all blurry and had a soft smile on his face. Even his vision wasn't clear, there wasn't a single trace of Project V. It was finally destroyed.

***

"I've got to hurry!" Keishla was desperately still running on her way to the rooftop. Moving as fast as she can, she jumped every obstacle on her way. She'd been trying to call for Zenrot but there was no answer. She hoped he didn't get behind. Finally reaching to the roof, the helicopter was arriving. Freddy was already waiting. "How did you get here so fast?" she gasped, trying to breathe.

"I found a shortcut."

"Next time tell me where it is."

Freddy looks around and saw someone was missing, "Where's Zenrot?"

"I don't know, he hasn't answered me back!" Keishla said, worried. She wanted to go back, but remembered everything was on lockdown. How was Zenrot going to get on the rooftop in time? Freddy suggested leaving while they still could—they had the intel, so it should be enough. The place was about to blow any minute, but she was in denial of leaving Zenrot.

Keishla tried to contact him again, again and again… no response. The pilot insisted to get in the helicopter and leave before the building exploded. Freddy climbed in, but Keishla was still outside on the roof waiting.

"Two minutes," she told the pilot, "and don't you dare leave. If he doesn't get here, we depart." Keishla tried to contact Zenrot one more time over the radio. "ANSWER ME, YOU DAMN BASTARD!"

"This is Zenrot," he finally spoke, *"target is neutralized."*

She had never felt so relieved hearing his voice. "Where the hell are you?"

"Still on floor twenty… trying to breathe."

"THIS IS NO TIME TO REST. This place will blow up in any moment. You must find a way, now!" The conversation went silent. She didn't hear anything in the background. "Do you hear me?" Keishla screamed into her communicator.

"Get in the helicopter," Zenrot gasped.

"The hell I'm leaving—"

"Listen to me…" He struggled to raise his voice, *"tell the pilot to circle the building around floor twenty. When you see a giant hole, get near to it and be ready."*

"Ready for what? Dark Boy, hello?" She immediately went

inside the helicopter and gave the pilot the instructions Zenrot gave to her. The pilot insisted they leave the building, but Keishla got very anxious and angry. She threatened the pilot by putting a dagger to his neck. "If you don't follow my orders, I will gladly slice your head off and use it as a voodoo figure."

Freddy slowly approached. "Keishla, I think we should reconsider—" A telekinetic dagger flew from her backpack and pointed directly at Freddy's face.

"We aren't reconsidering shit!" She fixed Freddy with an angry look then returned her attention to the pilot. "Start flying!" The pilot didn't question twice. The helicopter started orbiting around the building looking for the giant hole. "There! I see it, pull over there!" Keishla yelled at the pilot. The helicopter slowly moved into position.

She squinted her eyes enough to focus and finally saw Zenrot, struggling to stand. He must be exhausted because of the fight. Keishla yelled so he would see her, but no response. She asked the pilot to get closer but that was as far as he could get. Keishla knew he could get closer, but knew he wouldn't because he feared the explosion. She saw Zenrot standing and kept calling out to him.

"ONE MINUTE UNTIL SELF-DESTRUCT," a last warning sounded throughout the building.

"Dark Boy! Get your ass over here now!"

"He won't make it, let's get out of here now!" Freddy shouted and the pilot started slowly flying away.

She turned, frustrated. "Don't you dare leave! I will not leave him there to die! Even if I must—"

"Keishla, look!" Freddy shouted. She turned, looking back at the hole. Zenrot was coming in their direction; he was going to jump. The pilot wouldn't take the risk and started moving away from the building. As Zenrot ran, he put his sword on his back and his revolver on his waist. He sped up, running faster and faster.

"What are you doing? He's going to jump to the helicopter!"

"It's about 100 meters away! He won't make the jump," said the pilot.

"Oh yes he will!" Keishla looked around and found a rope, tying it off to a handle of the helicopter. She tied the other side of the rope around her waist.

"Are you insane? He won't make that jump," Freddy tried to talk to her out of it. "He's too far."

"Shut up!" Keishla walked a few inches back, ready to jump when it was time. Zenrot was getting closer to the jump. In three… two… one… Keishla ran and jumped as Zenrot passed the edge of the building. Seeing Keishla in the air, both stretched their arms to grab one another as they were falling all the way down, only inches away from grabbing the other's hands. As they fell, and just before the rope finally reached its end—

"GOTCHA!" Keishla grabbed Zenrot's hand. The rope went taut but prevented them from falling. "Get us out of here!" she yelled at the pilot, the helicopter already moving far away from the building. Freddy pulled them up as fast as he could.

BOOOOM! The building exploded and started collapsing to the ground. They had moved out of its blast radius in time.

"Frederick! Speed up, will you? My arm is getting tired!"

"I'm trying but you two are heavy as hell!"

"Are you calling me fat? Just wait until we get back to base!"

Freddy managed to pull them inside the helicopter. Keishla gently moved Zenrot, laying him on the floor while she looked for a med kit to tend to his wounds. Zenrot was still dizzy, but gave a weak smile. "Told you I'd be back, didn't I?" Keishla got furious and punched Zenrot in the arm. "Ow!"

"Don't you ever scare me like that again! Next time I'll let you die!"

Freddy laughed, "Funny, because you decided to risk all our lives to save him." He looked back to Zenrot. "That's her way of saying, 'glad to have you back.'"

Project V was gone, and they had recovered the intel they needed. The mission has been complete. All that was left was to return to Art Gun.

CHAPTER
EIGHT

Keishla was tending Zenrot's wounds using a bit of alcohol and medical antibiotic for the scars on his chest and the deep wounds on his arm. When Keishla touched his arms, Zenrot yelled in pain. The liquid Project V had released inside him was somehow still burning.

"Damn, he beat you pretty hard," she said with a sharp tone and sarcastic smile. "Next time you get the intel and I fight the target."

Zenrot chuckled. "There won't be another time, and I'm pretty sure you would've died in that fight." She squeezes his arm a bit. "Ow! Are you supposed to help me or not?"

"Not with that attitude," Keishla said while putting some bandages on his arm.

"Zenrot, I know what you're thinking, don't you say a word to her," Freddy warned as he started laughing softly. Zenrot was looking at his communicator, trying to contact Art Gun. Keishla was irritated because he wouldn't even take a break for himself.

"Zenrot reporting in. We have successfully eliminated Project V and got the intel you asked for on a device."

"*Copy that,*" Arashi answered, *"return to base safely. We have some other details to discuss. Right now, get some rest on your way, over.*"

"Copy that, over and out." Zenrot hung up and laid his head on the wall of the helicopter. Keishla sat next to him and showed the items she found in the lab back at Sentry Run's headquarters, starting with a pauldron. Zenrot grabbed it, looking over the piece and seeing the small needle attached to it. He also found the instructions on the side that read, *"STAB NEEDLE INTO YOUR RIGHT SHOULDER FOR FULL BODY ARMOR. MAKE SURE YOU'RE NOT WEARING ANY EQUIPMENT OR HAVE NEARBY OBSTACLES WHEN USED."* Keishla suggested this might be something to try on later, but Zenrot indicated he'd be happy to let Art Gun check on it first.

Freddy put his hand on his ear. Keishla noticed someone was talking to him through his communication device, then Freddy stood up and walked to speak with the pilot. Zenrot took the opportunity to speak privately with Keishla.

"I want to apologize, Keishla."

"Uh?" That took her by surprise. "For what? Being an asshole?"

"No," he answered flatly. "For putting you guys in danger. Because of my mistakes… Astred is gone. Everything would've gone better if I had listened to you about the vault. I should've done other choices. I should've—"

"Shut up," Keishla said. "Just… shut up. Please." Keishla

went silent and looked away, giving Zenrot the cold shoulder. He couldn't blame Keishla, but Zenrot wanted to know how she felt. Sadness? Anger? After all, Astred's last words were to look out for each other. The best thing for now was to give Keishla some space.

A few minutes later the helicopter changed directions and started shaking a bit.

"Where are we going?" Zenrot asked, confused.

"We're heading to Rasenof Forest," Freddy answered, walking back to them.

"That's few days on foot, far from Art Gun," Keishla said to Freddy.

"Arashi told me that we should take a day to rest before heading back. I explained Zenrot's condition, and he told me to lay low for the night."

"In the middle of a forest? That sounds safe," Zenrot said sarcastically. He tried to stand up, but it was still a struggle because of his wounds. Keishla forced Zenrot to rest and told him to stop thinking about giving orders. Zenrot insisted, but Keishla wasn't going to listen and told Freddy to speak with the pilot about finding a good landing spot in the forest.

When Freddy was out of earshot, Keishla whispered to Zenrot, making sure no one else listened. Zenrot gasped, surprise washing across his face as he looked at Keishla. She nodded with a finger on her lips, indicating to stay quiet.

The pilot found a clearing where there's a waterfall nearby and weren't many trees around for landing. When they reached the ground, Keishla helped Zenrot get off the helicopter. Freddy followed behind to set a campfire. The pilot stayed in the helicopter. Keishla took off her backpack for a small relief, and Zenrot took off his sword. She looked thoughtfully at the sword, got curious, and stood up to try and lift it. Unfortunately, it was too heavy for her.

"Holy shit! How is your back not ripped apart?" she yelled, struggling to at least *move* the sword. "Oh, screw it!" The boys started laughing together, and Freddy pointed out it was getting dark, then suggested everyone get some rest. He put his scythe next to Zenrot's sword, and Keishla added her backpack to the pile.

"Hey, pilot guy!" Freddy shouted. "You wouldn't have any pillows by any chance?" There was no response, but the pilot threw the backpack of a parachute. "I guess that can work."

Zenrot laughed and turned his gaze to Keishla. She only stared at Zenrot with a serious face; a reminder of what she had spoken. Keishla found a piece of tree trunk and decided to use that as a pillow. "Is that even comfortable?" Freddy asked.

"Mind your business." She laid on the forest floor, facing away and looking into the forest.

"*Sheesh.* I'm just asking if you'd prefer the backpack…"

"I'm fine," Keishla said. "Now let me sleep." Freddy didn't dare to speak to her and turned his eyes to Zenrot.

"It's been a hell of a journey," Zenrot commented. He slowly walked to a tree and gingerly turned himself around, lowering himself to the ground and resting his back against the tree.

"You need anything?" Freddy asked politely.

"*Agh!* I'm ok," Zenrot shouted briefly in pain while trying to get comfortable. "Just need some rest."

"All right." Freddy grabbed the parachute and puts it on the ground, laying himself down and getting comfortable. "Well, going to sleep. Good night."

"Night." Zenrot stayed awake, watching Freddy as he fell asleep. Zenrot wondered if the parachute would burn from the fiery ashes coming off of Freddy's head. His eyes swept the full perimeter, scanning the forest in case of ambush. About an hour later, nothing had happened. Zenrot's eyelids starts falling. He tried to stay awake, but he was exhausted from the battle. Everything looked blurry, until they finally shut, and fell asleep.

****

In the middle of the night, Zenrot heard a reckless noise. He stood up to look around, noticing the pilot was searching Keishla's backpack. Zenrot went to confront him.

"Everything all right?" he asked. The pilot jumped, scared. He tripped over his words, mentioning he lost something important, and thought Keishla might have taken it by accident. "Oh! Maybe I can help you. What is it exactly that you're looking for?" Zenrot politely asked.

The pilot started mumbling again, not knowing what to answer.

"You are searching for the device. Aren't you?" The pilot panicked, trying to deny it, but was speaking so nervously and, Zenrot noticed, sweating in fear. Keishla heard the noises and woke up.

"Uh, what's going on?" Keishla turned around, watching Zenrot and the pilot speaking, then noticing her backpack was open. "Who the hell is searching through my stuff?" she asked furiously, climbing to her feet.

"Apparently, this gentleman right here," Zenrot said calmly.

Keishla turned to face the pilot, taking a dagger out of her backpack with her telekinesis and pointing it in his face.

"Care to explain yourself?"

"What's all this about?" Freddy asked, coming over from a walk. He looked wide awake; apparently, he wasn't sleeping.

"He was searching through my stuff!" Keishla took a step forward to her backpack and the pilot ran to the helicopter. She then turned around to face Freddy. "But you would know about that… wouldn't you?"

"What are you talking—"

"Don't play dumb with me! You want the device, don't you? You were looking for the perfect chance to take it and leave us behind. You can't kill us, so you wanted to find an easy way to ditch us."

Freddy stayed quite for a good minute, not saying a word against her. Zenrot wasn't speaking until something occurred that he could judge. Freddy, on the other hand, transitioned from a face so serious and pale… to a smile. A smile that they could tell meant he was up to no good. "Well, well … to be honest, I thought Zenrot would've been the one to figure it out, not you, Keishla."

"I've known ever since you got to the roof before me. You didn't struggle your way up with all the Clambers in the way. You also insisted on leaving Zenrot many times. Lastly, I noticed back when we were flying that Arashi contacted you and gave instructions to the pilot. Yeah… even this dumb bitch has hidden tricks."

Freddy raised his hands, tilting his head down and walking very slowly toward them as he started laughing. "Congrats, you've caught me. Can't hide it no more. Unfortunately, I don't have much time to speak about it in detail. I am going to need that device, which—by the looks of it—the pilot couldn't find in your backpack. So, my guess is that *you* have it." He lowered his hands and turned his eyes up to Keishla. "If you can please—"

"Not going to happen," Zenrot interfered. His sword was a few steps away from being in reach. Zenrot was holding the gun on his waist, ready to take it out. Keishla slowly released her remaining daggers with her telekinesis.

"Trust me, this isn't a fight you want to pick. Hand over Astred's device. This is your final warning," he said politely. Zenrot held his gun tighter, and Keishla held her daggers in the air. An absolute silence settled between the three of them. Freddy closed his eyes and lowered his face, but his hair was igniting fast. His hands were already releasing fire. "Very well."

Freddy ran toward Zenrot first, since he was in the most vulnerable. His fists on fire, and close enough to punch Zenrot. Thanks to his great reflexes, Freddy dodge an incoming dagger. Turning to face Keishla, she had five remaining daggers. Freddy jumped away and Zenrot took the opportunity to reach for his sword, grabbing it with one hand and attack Freddy.

Zenrot swung his sword from above, but Freddy took the scythe and blocked the attack. He was impressed that Freddy could hold back the strength and the weight of the sword.

Freddy push Zenrot away with his scythe; quickly ran to get close, returning the scythe to his back. Up close, he punched Zenrot many times with his burning fists from the stomach up to the chest. Followed by jumping, flipping around, and kicking Zenrot in the face to take him down. Zenrot was on the ground groaning in pain, holding his stomach because of the burning punches.

"You may have strength, but I'm way faster than you." Freddy spoke confidently while releasing fire through his hand to finish Zenrot. Keishla surprisingly jumped in and kicked Freddy at the side of his arm, knocking him away. She started fighting Freddy up close. Both had the same reflexes and speed as they attacked hand to hand, parrying and blocking against each other.

"Why? Why the hell are you doing this? After everything we've been through?" Keishla shouted as she kept fighting. Zenrot was still on the ground watching the fight, where he noticed Keishla wasn't using her daggers against Freddy. On the other hand, Freddy didn't look like he would talk anytime soon.

Freddy grabbed Keishla by her ponytail, pulling her back hard. It made her bend, placing her off balance and off guard; Freddy attacked with his elbow, striking the center of her chest right between her breasts and forcing her to fall to the ground.

She growled in pain, but slowly stood back up. Freddy kicked Keishla with his boot, knocking her back to the dirt. He went through her pockets and found the device which had the intel stored on it. Standing, Freddy bent himself back to dodge an incoming energy bullet from Zenrot who was struggling just to keep his gun steady.

Freddy raised himself, turning to face Zenrot and giving a sharp smile. His hands were making fireballs and threw a couple to Zenrot. Zenrot raise his gun and started shooting the fire balls as he walked backwards. Having put enough pressure on Zenrot, Freddy ran ahead and turned his fists to fire. He gave a hard punch to Zenrot's stomach with his knuckles; Zenrot crouched, spitting curses. Freddy landed an uppercut on Zenrot's chin, however. As soon as Zenrot fell back, Freddy grabbed him with both hands. In a savage movement, he pulled Zenrot down and hit his face hard against Freddy's knee, making his nose bleed, and left him on the ground

The pilot was getting ready to depart with the helicopter.

"Frederick, let's go. We got what we needed. Finish them off!" he shouted from a distance. Freddy started walking to the helicopter while securing the device in his pocket.

"The hell… you're leaving." Struggling to speak, Keishla turned to push herself from the floor. Freddy got close to her and stomped her back against the ground with his foot. Then stomped a second time, making sure she didn't stand. Freddy slowly walked on his away. "You won't get away with this," she gasped, looking up as she watched him enter the helicopter.

"I believe I just did."

"What are you doing?" the pilot shouted. "You're supposed to leave no witnesses!"

"Bah! Quit your whining! They won't last here in the forest." Freddy tapped on his forehead, as if he had forgotten something. He slowly took out his scythe and turned around, taking a few steps to face Zenrot and Keishla. "By the way…" he said, waiting for Zenrot and Keishla to stand up. "You thought I couldn't kill you guys, right?" Freddy starts releasing fire through his scythe. "Let's put that to the test." He circled his scythe at incredible speed, creating a fire ring that slowly grew bigger. That's when Zenrot noticed his intention.

"Keishla… we must run, now!" He sounded frightened, slowly backing away.

"Why? We can take him," she said confidently, but still shaking from the hits. Keishla noticed Freddy's ring of fire was getting bigger than the size of the helicopter. She also walks backwards. "I take it back… RUN!" Keishla dashed to Zenrot and pushed him until they both made a run for it. Freddy completed the ring, forming a giant circle of fire. He threw it like a disk, igniting the whole forest. Trees became ashes in an instant while the fire spread, growing bigger as the seconds went by. The blaze grew close to Zenrot and Keishla. If they don't think of something soon, they'd be the next thing becoming ash. Zenrot looked around, searching for cover or anything to save them.

"Where do we go?" Keishla shouted, gasping.

They both caught sight of the waterfall ahead. Zenrot guessed it should be deep.

"How good is your breathing?" he asked, glancing at Keishla while they ran to the waterfall. Keishla was questioning the plan, but understood the idea as they approached. As soon as they reached the edge of the grass, they leapt from the cliff and dove into the water.

As their momentum was arrested by the water in the pool

under the waterfall, they could see the fire spreading across the top of it. They swam deeper in the water and tried to hold their breath until the coast was clear. After a few minutes had passed, they noticed a shadow pass overhead. It was Freddy.

He was looking around trying to find them. Keishla looked at Zenrot, fear visible on her face even in the half-light of the bottom of the pool. Zenrot put a finger to his lips, telling her to stay quiet and calm.

From deep under the water, Zenrot and Keishla heard the pilot speaking. "Did you eliminate them?"

"Definitely." Freddy confirmed their deaths, walking slowly around the edge of the pool one more time. Then he finally retreated to the helicopter.

When Zenrot and Keishla could no longer hear the blades of the helicopter, they swam to the surface. The pair finally got out, laying on the edge of the grass to breathe. Rasenof Forest was no more. Every tree were burning in flames, and the leaves were turning into ash. There was nothing green left—everything was gone.

"What the hell just happened?" Keishla coughed, spitting up water she had swallowed from being too long underwater.

"I think… we've just been banished from Art Gun."

CHAPTER
NINE

At midnight, Zenrot and Keishla were still walking away from the forest and heading in Art Gun's direction. They were looking for a place to crash for the night. The sky was cloudy and looked like it was going to rain. At least it will put out the fire that Freddy started back in Rasenof. After almost thirty minutes walking, they found a cave to sleep in. Soon after they got inside, it started raining. Zenrot and Keishla hadn't spoken to each other on their journey. Zenrot wanted to give Keishla space because he assumed she must be even more frustrated and confused than he was.

Siting in the cave, Zenrot removed the pieces of his armor, being extra careful to try not to touch his injuries. The gear had taken too much damage during their mission at Sentry Run's headquarters, so it had become useless to keep wearing the armor. Zenrot looked at his arm; the bandages were filled with blood. He wanted to remove the bandages to clean his arm, but Keishla saw his intent when he reached his other hand toward the knot.

"Don't even bother," she advised, "the wounds are too deep to remove the bandages now. If you take a wrong turn while sleeping, you'll start bleeding. Leave it until tomorrow."

He wasn't sure, but judging by the look on Keishla's face, she was being thoughtful about it; he deferred to her experience as she removed her backpack.

She climbed to her feet, removing her armor piece by piece and throwing it outside the cave. Looking at the state of her uniform, the small logo of Art Gun on the left side of her shirt catch her attention. Keishla took the sticks holding her hair up and let it fall loose. Zenrot looked closely, realizing they were thin knives. Keishla started slicing the logo from the shirt.

"You think that's a good idea?" Zenrot asked with an eyebrow raised, since the logo is above of her breast, and she was creating a hole in the fabric.

Keishla rolled her eyes. "I have a bra. So, you won't see anything—don't get any funny ideas." She pointed the knife at him.

"I wasn't!" Zenrot looked away.

She dropped the knife onto the shirt and gently started tearing the logo off, doing so carefully so the whole thing didn't unravel. "Besides, you think I'm going to represent these assholes after what happened?" Once she finished, she tied her hair into a ponytail and held it into place with the thin knives. "Question is, why'd they do this? And why'd Freddy try to kill us?"

"I don't know. I'm certain of one thing, though. Freddy could have killed us, but he let us live." Zenrot put his sword and gun to the side on the ground to make room to lay down. "Freddy knew we would've survived. My thought is he made that last attack to make the pilot believe we died."

"Uh… but why? Why would Freddy go to all that trouble? And why would Art Gun want us dead?"

"I wish I could answer those questions," Zenrot tried to get comfortable on the hard stone, "but we can't trust anyone from Art Gun right now."

"I say we go and find out ourselves!" Keishla demanded.

"Easy there, we're not in any condition to fight. Probably after today they will be more guarded than ever. We'll think this through tomorrow."

"Whatever." Keishla laid on the floor, turning to the side aggressively to view outside the cave, watching the smoke coming out of the forest. "I'm going to sleep," she said, struggling to find a comfortable way to lay. "For the record," she added softly, "I do not blame you for Astred's death. It wasn't your fault." She let those words hang in the still air of the cave and went silent. She had gone to sleep.

Zenrot was surprised Keishla brought that subject up. She had probably been holding on to it for a while, and hadn't known how to express herself about it until now. Zenrot was glad Keishla had spoken about it, and slowly laid down facing the ceiling of the cave. He tried to analyze everything that had brought them to this point, and wondered if Astred had been part of it. It didn't make sense that he would have been, as Astred was the one who had mentioned being aware of Art Gun before his death. Zenrot remembered Astred saying to stay with Keishla at all costs—he hadn't mentioned Freddy. Maybe Astred already knew something, but never had the time to say it. Zenrot was having doubts at those who had supported him: Mr. Han, Grim, Brandolf, and Ryan… especially Ryan. He was Zenrot's mentor, the one who had gifted him the sword, and had trained Zenrot to be who he is. Thinking about everything over and over, Zenrot finally fell asleep.

***

The next morning, the light of the sun crept inside the cave and touched Zenrot's face. He came awake, then looked to the side to see Keishla. She was still sleeping and, as he watched, started snoring—and a really heavy snore, at that.

"Such a delicate flower." he said, quietly sarcastic. Zenrot looked in her backpack, checking if there was any food to eat. *I'm going to regret this,* he thought. The daggers are stored in a compartment on the backpack, and the handles of each weapon are visible looking like a crown. Additionally, it featured a zipper that, when unzipped, could store a lot of underneath items. Lastly, there was a belt on the front that shut off a small pocket that held small items.

Zenrot opened the backpack and, apart from the daggers around it, found two pauldrons, four blades, a short staff, and a metal cord. *Why a string?* he thought. When Zenrot analyzed the blades and moved them closer, they connected to one another. Looking at the cord-like string and the short staff, Zenrot had an idea—an idea to work on a weapon. He remembered Keishla shooting at long range. Zenrot looked at his watch. 10:26 a.m. He would try his best to make the weapon by the end of the day.

A few hours passed and Keishla finally woke up. Her hair was all messy, even though it had been tied up with her thin knives. There was also drool on her face.

"Morning, sunshine," Zenrot lightly chided.

"Fuck off," Keishla said annoyed, scratching at her eyes to see better. "Did you search through my stuff?" Sleepiness was transitioning to anger as a dagger floated into the air.

"Sorry, you took a while to wake up and I got bored. So, I thought I'd make you something to help you fight in battle." Keishla gave Zenrot a dead stare but lowered her dagger and calmed herself down. She mentioned she'll go outside and walk around to see if she could find some food and water.

While Keishla was out of the cave, Zenrot continued working on the weapon. Two of the blades were short, and the other two were longer. Zenrot attached the blades to one side of the staff—one short with one long blade on each end, with the short side attached. He did the same thing with the other blades, creating a device to pull them in and out like a butterfly knife. The staff worked like a handle between the two blades.

After a few hours working, it was finally done.

He practiced a single gesture that caused the blade to pop open and shut closed with little effort. It wasn't hard to put the pieces together; it looked like the blades were made for that purpose, though the staff was improvised. Lastly, the string. Zenrot attached the metal cord to the tip of the blade and pulled it long enough to attach to the opposite tip. He made sure there was enough stretch to flex it into a bow.

Zenrot practiced with the gesture again, making sure the

cord didn't break. It retracted when the blades were pulled in and stretched enough to draw when the blades were out. After a few adjustments, Zenrot finally had the weapon how he wanted it. Just after he finished getting it ready, Keishla arrived.

"Man! There's barely anything in the area. Luckily, I found an apple tree. But there was only five." Keishla handed two apples to Zenrot.

"You only brought four."

"I ate one on the way." Her eyes drifted to the weapon in his hand. "What is that?"

"It's a knife bow." Zenrot explained the custom weapon, and how he had made it to operate in both close and ranged combat. Keishla was impressed with Zenrot's work.

"Would it be a new toy of yours?" she asked, underplaying her interest in the device. Zenrot tried not to laugh because he found Keishla adorable; by the look on her face, she obviously liked the weapon.

"No, I made it for you," Zenrot said, stretching his arm out and holding the knife bow out for her.

"Wait! You're serious?" She was surprised.

"Take it, it's yours. Besides, I made it with the items *you* found. It's only fair. Also, because it isn't my style. I know you like to fight silently, and I've heard you've got good aim. So, take it, it's yours," Zenrot insisted.

After moments of consideration, she finally took it. Smiling, admiring the weapon from different angles, Zenrot could tell Keishla was happy. He sat down to take a break and eat his apple. After a moment, Zenrot looked up to Keishla. "Tomorrow

I would like to see how your aim is."

Keishla looked at him with confusion. "How do you want me to shoot it? I don't have arrows."

"I think I can make a few within the forest… if there's any branches left." Zenrot suggested he could craft some arrows, but even if he made plenty of them, it wouldn't be enough to fight off an army. Zenrot was thinking for other solutions when—

He snapped his fingers, coming up with an idea for Keishla.

"Or maybe… you use your energy…"

"Uh?" Keishla was even more confused. "I don't follow."

"You can use your energy to make your own arrows. Just like I do with my gun. That way you have unlimited ammunition—at least until you run out of energy."

Keishla laughed nervously, thinking it was a joke, but the way Zenrot spoke was damn serious. "I—I can't. I find it very difficult to release energy like that."

"But I've seen you releasing energy in the blade of your daggers and the sword."

"It's not that simple," Keishla said, sounding embarrassed. "I always focus my energy with my telekinesis. I can only lift lightweight objects, and very specific ones. It's easy to release my energy through the daggers because I'm used to always fighting with them." Keishla stared at her hand, trying to release energy from her fingers. Only spikes of light came out. "Other than my blades, when I try to release my energy to create an ability of my own… I feel like something inside my body is preventing its release." Keishla looked at Zenrot. "It sounds strange but is the truth."

"Mmm… maybe you need to practice with the knife bow from now on." Zenrot took out his gun, moving carefully because of his injuries. "You could try practicing like Ryan taught me back during my training. Honestly, I never learned how to release my energy like Frederick. But when Ryan had this gun made for me, it made it a lot easier. It was designed as a way to use energy, but without needing the control required to release freely without hesitation. Think of it as a way to train the body in what it feels like to have to sustain your own energy."

"Ryan sounds like a good trainer."

"He was…" Zenrot turned to look back at his sword. "I just hope he isn't involved in this mess." Zenrot's eyes unfocused and he stared blankly forward while he ate his second apple. Keishla felt a bit sad because she could tell that Zenrot really cared for the major.

"We'll get answers soon. I promise," Keishla said.

"Yeah…" he sounded uncertain. Zenrot finished his apple and noticed it was getting dark. While he was preparing to sleep inside the cave, a question occurred to him. "By the way… did you have any specific plans with the string before I used it?" As he laid himself on the ground, Zenrot looked at Keishla curiously. Even though she had received the knife bow enthusiastically, Zenrot felt a twinge of guilt for having taken the parts and used them without having asked first.

Keishla laughed sarcastically, apparently unconcerned.

"Well, I was planning to use it as a weapon to strangle someone with, but you made it so much more useful." Zenrot smiled nervously, thinking about the strange ways which Keishla chose to eliminate her enemies. She tried to change the subject. "Anyways, you must be tired from working on this weapon all afternoon. Get some rest. I'll sleep in a few minutes."

Keishla sat at the entrance of the cave and looked at the stars. She could sense Zenrot was still awake—possibly because he was afraid Keishla would betray him in his sleep. Keishla turned her head a little, looking back at Zenrot and noticing he was looking back at her.

"Don't worry. I won't kill you in your sleep for touching my stuff," she said softly, winking at Zenrot. He laughed nervously, turned himself over, and tried to sleep. Keishla chuckled and turned to look back at the stars. Even after all the mess of these last several days, she was enjoying the quiet moments of a peaceful night.

CHAPTER
TEN

It was daylight. Zenrot was on the waterfall near Rasenof Forest, which there wasn't much left of it. Luckily, the rain did stop the fire from spreading. In a few years, the forest may grow back the way it was. Zenrot had his shirt off and was carefully removing his bandages. He gently cleaned the blood away from his arm. He could see the small holes Project V had left with its claws. The same went for his stomach. It wasn't bad like his arm. After that, Zenrot grabbed his shirt and put it back on as he stood up. Still shrugging into his shirt, he was abruptly pushed from the back, falling into the waterfall. He swam to the top, ready to attack.

"Morning, Sunshine." It had been Keishla smiling, who pushed Zenrot.

"The hell was that for?" Zenrot asked.

"So, you can clean yourself properly. You stink."

"Very funny." Zenrot shook his hands and twisted water out of his shirt. He noticed that Keishla had the knife bow in her hand.

"So. You have any tricks on releasing energy from your hands?" Keishla asked.

Zenrot chuckled and walked over. "Well, let's get to it." He took his gun from his holster. Zenrot showed Keishla how he focused his energy through the palm of his hand, and how it slowly flowed from there to inside the cylinder. Zenrot suggested concentrating on an object, in this case, her knife bow. It was not the exact same method as Zenrot's revolver, because Keishla would have to create an arrow with her energy.

She found that difficult to do, so for starters she took a thin knife out from her hair, and it fell lose. Keishla tried to focus her energy on the blade. She slowly formed a new shape with her energy, forming the blade longer and sharper. Once Keishla felt the energy flowing through the blade she dropped the weapon, pulling at the energy with her fingers. She kept it in the palm of her hand, carefully starting to shape the energy into the form of an arrow. She started to stretch the knife shape out, to better resemble the shaft, and—

It exploded. "Fuck!" Keishla shook her hand, then angrily grabbed the thin knife from the ground.

"It's all right, you're getting the hang of it. Keep focused," Zenrot encouraged. Keishla tries again, this time attempting it without the knife. She deftly wound it back into her hair to hold the ponytail, then opened her hand flat. Keishla freely, slowly released her energy and formed the arrow once again. After a few seconds, however, it turned into a small ball of energy and exploded.

"Shit!" she screamed, waving her hand up and down. "I

don't know how you do it with your gun."

"Here," Zenrot handed the revolver to Keishla, "try my gun, then."

Keishla hesitated to grab it but wrapped her hands around the handle of the revolver and took it anyway.

"Aim for that tree," Zenrot pointed with his finger, "try releasing your energy slowly. Let it flow into the handle of the gun."

Keishla held it with two hands, slowly releasing energy from her palms. Her energy slowly traveled through the handle, charging the weapon. Zenrot noticed something in the process.

"Your energy is yellow," he said softly.

"Something bad about that?"

"No. Just an observation."

Keishla could feel the gun was loaded enough. She take the shot, and her energy burned through the air all the way to the tree, breaking into pieces. Zenrot watched Keishla and noticed how shooting with his gun exhausted her quickly.

"I suggest you practice with the revolver," Zenrot said, "that way you can develop your resistance in using your energy. When you feel confident enough, you can try to create an arrow from scratch."

"Never knew it would be this difficult…"

"It's only a matter of practice. It took me a while to get used to it." Zenrot walked away into the forest.

"Where are you going?"

"I'm going to make a few arrows since this might take some time. You keep practicing."

"*Pfft*. Easier said than done…"

***

Keishla had been practicing for about two hours with Zenrot's revolver. It was difficult to control her energy like Zenrot, but she managed to learn her limits very well. Zenrot was sitting on a boulder, watching how Keishla practiced with regular arrows he had made for her. She was looking at the remaining trees, giving all her attention to the leaves. As a few started to fall, took out an arrow and shot at a leaf, cutting through it. She looked at three more falling, running around in a circle with her knife bow in hand and ready to shoot. Finally, she took the shot. It hit the three leaves with a single arrow.

"Not bad." Zenrot was amazed. "You do have good aim."

"*Heh*. It's nothing," Keishla said, a bit cocky. "Think I should give it another try with the energy arrow thing?"

"Think you can handle it?" Zenrot said with a smirk on his face.

"Now you're just being a dick."

"Just try, already."

Keishla turned her back and saved the other arrows on her backpack. She opened her hand in front of her and slowly started releasing energy. She delicately shaped it into a small ball. The energy was steadier, but the ball quickly disappeared. "Ah! Come on!"

"At least it didn't explode this time. It's a start."

"Still! It's getting annoying."

"Try again. Do your best to focus."

Keishla took a deep breath and tried again. It gradually formed into a ball. Keishla flicked a finger, trying to keep the energy steady, and noticed that the ball got a bump from the motion. She had the idea to move her fingers as her ball started taking shape. Zenrot was surprised her energy was lasting that long.

"That's it! Keep it going!"

"Shh! Focusing."

Keishla kept playing with her fingers until the energy ball got a complete shape and finally transform into an arrow. Keishla stood steadily, closed her fingers until she grabbed the arrow.

There was no explosion. The energy didn't disappear. She had created it.

"Awesome, you did it!" Zenrot jumped from the boulder to congratulate her.

Keishla gave a weak smile, but deep down she was excited. She didn't want to show her emotions in front of Zenrot. Keishla fell back to a familiar, cold expression.

"Where do you want me to shoot?" she asked.

Zenrot looked around to find any suitable target. He found a few rocks on the ground, about eight inches long, and grabbed six of them. Indicating Keishla to shoot while they were in the air, Zenrot threw one rock, about a hundred meters away. Keishla immediately raised her bow, forming an energy arrow and shooting. She blew up the rock with a direct hit.

"Nice aim. Let's try another." Zenrot threw another rock further away—about five hundred meters. Keishla held an energy arrow with the knife bow, focusing on the rock before it reached the ground. A few seconds later she took the shot. Another direct hit.

"Nice!"

"Pfft! Throw more rocks at the same time."

"All right. This time I'll throw them high. Think you can see them through the leaves?"

"Try me."

Keishla felt confident and Zenrot smiled while throwing the last four rocks sky high. Keishla aimed upwards, using her telekinetic daggers to cut most of the leaves and branches out of her way. She had one eye closed and the other one trying to spot the rocks. After a few seconds, she spotted the rocks and shot multiple times, destroying every single one of them. It sounded like fireworks.

The records back in Art Gun were not wrong, Keishla was good at shooting long range. Zenrot asked if she could use her telekinesis with the knife bow, but Keishla mentioned she had already tried it. She explained that it felt too heavy for her, and reminded Zenrot that she only could lift very lightweight objects with her telekinesis.

"Let me guess, you wanted to see if I could control the bow and shoot while moving it around through the air?"

"Honestly, that'd be damn cool." Zenrot returned the revolver to his holster. He slowly stretched his injured arm, moving it in different directions to regulate the pain. He looked up to Keishla. "Tomorrow we should train a bit to warm up, then we go to Art Gun and seek answers."

"You sure about this?" Keishla asked with a raised eyebrow.

"You know they'll try to kill us."

"Perhaps. But remember, we fought against an army of robots and strange experiments. This won't be any different."

"Except that we're going to kill many people who we used to trust." Zenrot flinched when Keishla said it out loud. The people he used to trust… Ryan.

There were also civilians Zenrot and Keishla had rescued from different cities back when the MSF started. Many lives would be at stake. Once they reach Art Gun's base, Arashi and his men won't want to have a chat about their actions—Zenrot and Keishla would have to fight until death. Zenrot didn't like the idea of attacking the base or taking the lives of people who were supposed to stand for the mutant cause. Maybe not everyone was as good as Art Gun described themselves to be, but deep down Zenrot also knew not everyone was bad either. Keishla, however, thought differently. Zenrot could tell what she wanted by the look in her eyes. Revenge.

"So," Keishla said, "are we going to kick some ass?"

"We will head to Art Gun and demand answers," Zenrot sighed. "On one condition," he instructed. Keishla questioned what Zenrot would ask for. "We will not kill any civilians." Zenrot noticed she didn't like where he was heading. "Regardless of what Art Gun just did to us. Our business is with Art Gun only, not with anyone else. I despise that we will have to kill soldiers, but we have no other choice. However, killing innocent people is out of the question."

"Even if they preached for Art Gun?" Keishla asked. "It's only a matter of time before they turn against us as well.

Remember, most people don't like mutants. Some humans will gladly help Art Gun even if they're the bad ones. Just to kill us."

"Perhaps you're right," Zenrot admitted. "But we're not doing this for revenge. We're doing this because it's the right thing to do." Zenrot stretched his arm to Keishla with an open hand. "Do we have a deal?" She only stared at his hand. It seems she didn't liked Zenrot's conditions. She looked at him directly at his eyes.

"I'll help you against Art Gun. After we finish our mission, we part ways. You have good intentions, Dark Boy, but those good intentions have consequences. I'd rather be alone. No friends. No family. No distractions. It's the only way people like us can survive against this accursed world."

Zenrot sniffed, staring back at Keishla. "Honestly, I find that hard to believe." He brightly smiled. "But if that's what you want, I'm fine with it."

Keishla scoffed. She was surprised Zenrot could be so full of hope and motivated to do what he saw as right. She looked at Zenrot's hand, playing with her fingers and trying to decide if the best choice was to accept the deal. After a quick thought, she shook his hand.

"All right! Looks like we're all set." Zenrot smirked, pulled Keishla in, and—with his other hand—calmly pushed her into the waterfall. Swimming back up to the surface, Keishla furiously glared at Zenrot.

"The fuck was that for?"

"You needed a shower. Because you stink," Zenrot chuckled. "Also, because karma is a bitch." He winked and she removed the thin blades from her hair, and throw them at Zenrot. He dodged by moving his body to the side, swinging one leg back.

"You missed—Ouch!" The knives each made a small cut on the side of Zenrot's arm before they returned to Keishla, floating casually.

"Next time will be your head." Keishla swam to the edge and climbed out of the water, putting her knife bow in the ground. "Get out of here, will you?" She was annoyed. "I'm going to dry these clothes, plus take some time in the waterfall while waiting.

"And what am I supposed to do?" Zenrot touched his shirt, then his pants. "My clothes are a bit soaked."

"That's a *you* problem." Keishla sat on the ground taking off her boots and socks. "Go back to the cave and take your clothes off there. Let them dry outside if you must. Don't you dare come back to the waterfall unless I've gone back to the cave." Keishla took off her shirt. With only a dark bra covering her torso, Zenrot noticed the multitude of cuts and bruises on her skin. He could tell some were recent, while others were from a long time ago. "Got it?" she asked.

"Yeah, got it," he replied. Keishla stood up, undoing her belt and proceeding to take off her military-issue pants. "Question... how can I be certain you won't check on me when I'm drying my clothes?" He was asking in the manner of a joke.

Keishla, however, stopped lowering her pants, and gave the deadliest of stares to Zenrot. He noticed Keishla wasn't in the mood for jokes any longer.

"Right, bad joke. I'm out."

***

About three hours had passed. Zenrot was outside near the cave he and Keishla were staying in. His clothes were near a rock, drying in the bright sunlight. While he waited, Zenrot was practicing going from one point to another, using his inner energy reserves on his feet to improve his running. He noticed Keishla ran at maximum speed when she used energy on her feet. However, Zenrot was experiencing quite the opposite. It seemed like his legs were being sucked into the ground. He had already mastered running faster than an average person, but nothing close to Keishla. Even back at Art Gun, when they took the night out to escape from the base, Keishla had been way ahead. Zenrot tries one more time, he took a bad step and fell, slowly standing back up.

"What are you doing?" Keishla asked as she walked over, wearing her uniform.

"Practicing my speed. I need to run faster if I want to keep up against the soldiers."

"Two things. One, you don't want to use your energy on your feet *before* running. Two," Keishla grabbed Zenrot's hand to help him stand, "will you please train with your clothes on?"

"Oh! Sorry." Zenrot jogged over to grab his clothes. He pulled his uniform and boots back on and, once Zenrot was ready, Keishla explained how she controlled her energy within her feet. She shared that she only used it when she's already sprinting. More specifically, she used her energy after she was running regularly to quickly speed up. It made her feel like she was running on air. However, she also cautioned that she only used a slight amount of energy. If she used too much, she'd stick to the ground—just like Zenrot had been experiencing while practicing on his own.

Keishla runs around Zenrot, telling him to focus on her feet. While slowly running, she hadn't used any energy. Speeding up, Zenrot noticed Keishla's energy was faintly visible on her feet. She continued to speed up and see that she had kept the same amount of energy in her feet, despite the increase in speed. Later, she stopped.

"Now you try it." Keishla spoke.

Zenrot started running and as he increased his speed, it started releasing energy. He felt more lightweight as he ran.

"Nice. You're getting the hang of it very quickly." Keishla congratulated. Zenrot being proud he tried to stop and fell to the ground.

"Ouch!" Zenrot shouted. "Felt like stopping in quicksand."

"You'll get used to it," Keishla said as she walked to the cave. "Let's get some rest. Tomorrow we should head to Art Gun. It will probably take us a few days of walking."

***

The next morning, Zenrot and Keishla were in the cave gathering their belongings and getting ready to go to Art Gun.

"Wait," she directed just before leaving and took out the pauldrons she still had in her backpack. She gave one to Zenrot. "We will face countless enemies when we get to Art Gun. If these things work for our protection, we should give it a try." Zenrot looked at the device; he wasn't convinced it was safe to use.

Keishla read the instructions. "*STAB NEEDLE INTO YOUR RIGHT SHOULDER FOR FULL BODY ARMOR. MAKE SURE YOU'RE NOT WEARING ANY EQUIPMENT OR HAVE NEARBY OBSTACLES WHEN USED.*"

"What do you think?" Keishla said uncertainly as she looked at him with her eyebrows raised.

Zenrot put his sword and gun away, and made sure he was not wearing any gadgets.

"Only one way to find out." Zenrot opened the device by pulling the needle out and stabbed himself on the right shoulder. The device turned on, flashing a red light, as the veins on Zenrot's body became visible. The piece started multiplying over his body and face. The pieces started molding, adjusting to his size. When it finally finished, Zenrot walked to Keishla feeling a little heavier. He looked over his arms and legs, which were covered in black carbon metal armor with small red neon lines accentuating it. Zenrot tried to touch his face, but felt he was wearing a helmet.

"So, how does it look?"

"You look badass! Why did we take so long to use this?" She shrugged out of her backpack and put her sword and knife bow down quickly. She grabbed her pauldron and used it on herself. It was the same armor, but the neon accents on her suit were violet. Keishla had trouble with her helmet because of the hair accumulated inside, but quickly found a way by making a small hole at the back of the helmet so she could take out her ponytail. "Well, the armor works like any ordinary armor."

"Looks like these were made for soldiers who needed a quick

cover for their body," Zenrot observed as he stretched his arms. He kept moving around, trying to feel the comfort and mobility of the armor. "They used great material."

"But it's a pain in the ass to wear," Keishla spit out and put the helmet back on.

"This can withstand many impacts. But we must not get too comfy on the battlefield either." Zenrot looked at his right shoulder and found a small red button. He pushes it with his finger and the armor starts retracting away back into the Pauldron. Zenrot retrieved his sword and gun and headed outside. Keishla did the same with the pauldron and picked up her stuff to follow Zenrot. Both left the pauldron on their shoulders. "We'll head on our way. Art Gun must know about the armor and many other things thanks to that device. If they tried to kill us already, who knows what else they might have planned for later."

"Oh, I know they don't have a plan to face us, and as for Freddy… I'm going to teach him a lesson when we find him." Keishla walked next to Zenrot. "Besides, we're in this together now, right?" She tapped him on his right arm.

"So that means we're officially friends?"

"Oh, Dark Boy," Keishla said, while she tapped on his head to mock him and got pushed away. "At this point, of course we are. However, when we're *officially real* friends, I'll call you by your real name." She took a few steps forward and looked back over her shoulder, "Let's get going, you're leading the way."

"Very well. Let's go." Zenrot started running ahead and Keishla followed. They were on their way to fight against Art Gun.

CHAPTER
ELEVEN

After days of running at maximum speed and resting from time to time, Zenrot and Keishla were meters away from Art Gun's entrance, hiding behind the trees. Art Gun's defenses had increased ever since they'd got Astred's electronic device. Robots just like the Golem and Spartans, except painted in the red and black of Art Gun's colors. Soldiers with stronger equipment and upgraded weapons guarded the entrance. Keishla looked for any other entrance, but the walls outside the base were extremely high with guns and sensors in case someone tried to climb. Art Gun would to take down Zenrot and Keishla if they tried to go over the wall.

"Well… climbing isn't an option," Keishla said, "unless we want to blow up like popcorn. Guess we're going to throw a welcome party at the entrance." She turned to Zenrot and asked confidently, "You ready?" He didn't immediately respond; she noticed he seemed bummed out. "What's wrong, Dark Boy?"

Zenrot breathed heavily, feeling doubt at almost everything.

"I know it's the worst time… but I can't stop wondering if Major Ryan was involved in all this. After all he did for me, I can't imagine he would betray me like that. He made me who I am today and—I just don't know what to believe anymore."

Keishla knew it was not easy. Zenrot really cared about Ryan, just as she had for Astred. She didn't want to make a joke about it. Instead, she slid close to Zenrot and touched his shoulder. "I don't think he did." Zenrot lit up, looking up at Keishla. "Probably… he was forced by Arashi or something. But the only way to find out is to beat the hell out of these bastards we once called our comrades." Keishla pushed the button of her pauldron, covering her whole body with armor. "So let's find some answers, shall we?"

A smile grew across Zenrot's face. No one knew for sure what could've happened inside Art Gun, but he was glad to hear there was still hope. He pushed the button on his pauldron, allowing the armor to unfold. "Hell yeah, we will."

Zenrot and Keishla turned to face Art Gun's entrance. Both ran with massive speed at the four soldiers and four robots that were on guard. Keishla went ahead and killed the soldiers with her telekinetic daggers while Zenrot shot two of the robots in their heads. He swiftly pivoted to stab the third robot with his sword, then withdrew it to slice through the last one. As soon as they had eliminated the defenses at the entrance, an alarm sounded throughout the Art Gun base.

"Well, we got their attention."

Zenrot checked if their communicators were still working and tried to contact Arashi. "Evening. Is General Arashi available?"

"The hell is going on?" someone answered—probably one of Arashi's bodyguards. *"Who is this?"*

"I think you know who it is. We're coming for you Arashi, and we want answers."

"No! That's impossible…" There was another intense voice. The voice of a man frustrated at hearing Zenrot: Arashi. *"You're supposed to be dead!"*

"Well, your soldier Frederick Crossvelt didn't get the job done. You better be ready. Zenrot out."

"You son of a—" Zenrot cut the call and changed frequency to speak only between him and Keishla. After Zenrot's message, Arashi sent countless numbers of troops. Every building was covered with close combat and ranged soldiers pointed at the main entrance. Soldiers started shooting at Zenrot and Keishla, but the bullets weren't doing any damage because of their armor. They sprinted through the gunfire to the closest soldiers, separating from each other as they ran. Zenrot killed his way through the soldiers on one side while Keishla did the same on the other.

Zenrot communicated with Keishla over the radio.

"Will be better if we split, you take the left side of the base, I'll take the right. Clear everyone on your way and we'll meet at Art's Grill." Zenrot ran ahead, seeing soldiers firing with their rocket launchers. As he ran at great speed, Zenrot dodged the bullets and explosives and swung his sword. He attacked the closest soldiers, cutting them in half with one swing. He shot the enemies in the distance with his revolver, passing an energy beam through their bodies.

Zenrot's thoughts felt disconnected from his body as he had the realization that he was murdering actual people; something he hadn't wanted to commit. A soldier from afar took an opportunity while he was still and shot Zenrot in the hand with a rifle. He dropped the sword, feeling pain in the hand. Luckily, the armor was strong enough to prevent the bullet from penetrating deeply. With his other hand, Zenrot aimed and shot the soldier with a high energy beam, blowing him into pieces. As he shifted his weight to keep running forward, Zenrot was hit by a truck.

The impact of the vehicle threw him to the ground, rolling rapidly, but he quickly recovered enough to stand. He heard more vehicles approaching at his back; two more trucks with soldiers getting out and aiming their rifles.

"There's nowhere to go, Zenrot!" a soldier shouted. "We've got you surrounded!"

"We have your sword!" Another soldier shouted. The soldiers were slowly approaching. As one soldier got closer, Zenrot chuckled.

"Looks like you can't do shit without a weapon in your hands."

Zenrot holstered his revolver, stretched his knuckles, and slowly turned around.

"You're dead wrong," Zenrot responded angrily. He jumped on the soldier that had spoken, giving one single punch to the soldier's stomach. He used the mouthy soldier as a human shield as he rotated in a circle shooting the rifle. He killed all the soldiers in the way and threw the last one to the ground. He smashed him in the face with the stock of the rifle repeatedly until the soldier's head was squashed. Zenrot ran to grab his sword and headed on his way.

On the other side of the base, Keishla rushed into a group of soldiers. Everyone started shooting at her, but she blocked every incoming bullet with her daggers using telekinesis and slicing them into literal pieces with her sword. Their arms, legs, and heads floated into the air behind her as she worked her way through the group. Keishla returned her sword to its scabbard and noticed something shining in the distance. Sniper soldiers. Keishla was moving too fast for them to easily keep track of her. Running to their location, she jumped and ran up the building. She eliminated each sniper by stabbing them in the head.

As the weapons floated back to Keishla's backpack, someone shouted, "She's in the tower, fire!"

Keishla looked down as she was running from the building, seeing soldiers with RPG-7s. Everyone shot at the same time. Keishla stopped and let herself fall. Rockets from the RPG passed her side as she fell, blasting apart the upper portion of the building. She maneuvered her fall close to the building, running the rest of the way down as it slowly crumbled.

Keishla jumped to the soldiers' location, releasing all her daggers on her way down. The swarm of blades sliced every soldier's neck. She used her telekinesis to recover all her daggers and save them in her backpack. Keishla saw a new army from afar. They are divided into two squads, one coming for Zenrot and the other moving in her direction.

"You see that?" she communicated with Zenrot, keeping her voice quiet.

"I see them. The plan is still the same, eliminate everyone on your way." He sounded so serious that it surprised her. Keishla drew her main dagger, splitting it into two and taking one in each hand. The rest of her daggers floated around.

The army was closing in, including the Spartans. Apparently they received special customization from Art Gun. They have been built with stronger metal, and on one hand they had a lance. When they hit it on the ground, high-voltage electricity arced from the weapon. In their other hand was a thicker iron shield that could handle heavier impacts than before.

"Finally, a real challenge." Keishla was excited, she rushed to the Spartans and attacked the first one, but she was pushed back by the shield and got electrified. She bounced on the floor, but quickly stood up.

"Now I'm really mad!" She said.

"Are you all right?" Zenrot asked over the radio.

"Oh, never better!" Keishla directed all her daggers at one Spartan. As it was defending itself, Keishla approached from behind and, with her knife bow, cut through its head. She pivoted and attack the rest.

Zenrot shot the Spartan in his side. They gathered to block every one of his shots with their shields. They drew their lances, charging them with electricity and shooting voltage at Zenrot, he dodged and jumped away. However, the five Spartans were running in straight lines toward him. Zenrot shot a massive burst of dark energy with his revolver to wipe them out. The Spartans blocked the energy bullet and instantly sent it back to Zenrot. He leaped to one side to dodge it.

Zenrot communicated to Keishla, "Looks like Art Gun's been busy with the intel they got from Astred's device. Be on guard from unexpected attacks—who knows what other upgrades they did to these Spartans, or any other threats," Zenrot jumped very high, charging his revolver while falling in the center of the Spartans. He took the shot and blow them away.

Keishla grabbed her knife bow and ran while shooting energy arrows at each Spartan. Hitting them directly in their heads and the robots fell to the floor. However, even once disabled, one of them released a shockwave. Keishla, being all surprised, reacted quickly and got away.

"Oh, they have upgraded all right," she radioed Zenrot. "Luckily, we have our armor, though. I assume they have bigger gadgets waiting for us, so we must be vigilant."

"Agreed, this will get heavy. Arashi must be shitting himself by now."

Zenrot and Keishla came into the same area. They had managed to reunite once again. Both heard a strange noise and looked in the same direction. Far off still, but heading to their location, there were hundreds of Project Clambers as Keishla identified them.

"Well, we got more coming now."

"I thought these were bad creations of—you-know-what," Keishla said, avoiding speaking the actual name.

"I bet they saved these Clambers in case they needed to create their own prototype for the battlefield." The Clambers were getting closer and soldiers from different ranks were waiting for orders. There were so many enemies to handle.

Zenrot looked around and saw dead bodies from enemies he had killed on the way. He snapped, "I have a plan, make sure no one gets close to me," and rushed to one of the dead bodies. He grabbed an RPG-7 from the ground and looked for a tall building. Seeing something that met his need nearby, he started climbing all the way to the top. Keishla was confused about what Zenrot was trying to do. "On my signal," Zenrot's voice crackled through the communicator, "you get away from the army as fast as you can."

Keishla saw Zenrot with the RPG-7 at the top of the building and instantly understood of his plan. Zenrot pointed at the army and started charging his revolver with his energy. The Clambers crawled desperately towards his location.

Keishla moved ahead. "All right, let's dance a little!" She rushed into the mass of Clambers with the knife bow and the daggers floating in the air around her. She did her best to fight the Clambers at a distance, cutting them into pieces and shooting her energy arrows to finish them off. While Keishla cut through the Clambers, though, some left acidic liquid on the floor, melting away at the ground. Other portions of the severed Clambers were forming into multiple mini-Clambers, which crawled to Keishla and jumped onto her. Their faces had sharp metal teeth, and the creatures repeatedly bit her armor. Their bites slowly melted it.

With her smallest dagger, she tried to cut them off before they melted her armor completely. "What's taking you so long?" Keishla shouted to Zenrot, angry and desperate. "These Clambers are a problem for our suits! Better hurry up with your plan."

Zenrot replied, exhausted, "I'm almost there, just a little longer." He was breathing hard as he continued charging his revolver.

The soldiers noticed one was missing from the fight against the Clambers. They looked around to find Zenrot and, after a minute, one of the soldiers noticed he was on top of the building.

"Above!" the soldier shouted in a panic. "And he's charging a weapon. Everyone, target Zenrot right now!" The soldiers aimed and started shooting at the top of the building.

"Oh no you don't, boys!" Keishla yells furiously. She removed most of the mini-Clambers from her armor and ran back through the horde on her way to Zenrot. Keishla used her telekinetic daggers to parry the incoming bullets toward him. Then, with the knife bow, she started shooting energy arrows, hitting a couple of soldiers to keep them distracted.

Running up the walls, Keishla quickly reached the top next to Zenrot. "What's wrong? Is the energy bullet too strong for you? Hurry up!" Then Keishla jumped her way down, continuing to parry the bullets coming for Zenrot.

She reached the ground and rushed into the middle of the army. Slashing one by one with the knife bow, and few soldiers had the guts to join close combat against Keishla. She stabbed the knife bow against the ground, fighting them hand to hand. She knocked them out of the way and with her daggers blocked incoming bullets, but some managed to hit her armor. While she was fighting, she noticed more soldiers and Clambers coming.

"There's so many of them! I can't hold on much longer. Are you ready?" Keishla yelled at Zenrot over the radio.

"Yes! GET OUT OF THE WAY!" Zenrot screamed.

Keishla ran incredibly fast, cheetah-like, away from the army. Zenrot fired with the RPG. As the rocket streaked downward, Zenrot quickly raised his revolver and aimed at the RPG's projectile.

"This is going to be a mess…"

Zenrot took the shot, the energy bullet on course to the rocket before it would hit the ground. When the energy hits the explosive, a massive explosion tore through the entire section. Zenrot's energy expanded the explosion, vaporizing all the Clambers and soldiers, even the buildings around the area started collapsing.

Keishla kept running, she could feel the intensity of the explosion. Finding cover, she looked to where Zenrot was located. He wasn't on the rooftop any longer. After a moment, she saw him at ground level, slowly walking to her destination. Looking at him across the distance, Zenrot raised his hand with a thumbs up. It was a sign for Keishla to keep moving. They weren't far away from Art's Grill location.

Keishla was the first to get close. She noticed the windows were broken, chairs were flipped, and tables were cracked. She assumed Zenrot's explosion was responsible. Keishla walked inside and found two chairs next to one another, close to the cabinet that now only housed broken plates, cups, and the like. A few seconds later, Zenrot arrived, sitting heavily next to Keishla. Both breathed deeply and took a moment to rest.

"Is it me," Keishla gasped, "or is there not a single civilian inside the base?"

Zenrot hadn't noticed it but realized Keishla was right. They hadn't seen any civilians since they got inside Art Gun.

"Probably knew we survived and called for an evacuation plan," Zenrot suggested.

"It doesn't make sense," Keishla disagreed. "Freddy tried to kill us. He thought we died back in Rasenof. So there is no point for evacuation if they believed we died."

"Like I said before," Zenrot took off his helmet, "I believe Freddy let us live. Question is… why all the trouble?" He turned to look at Keishla. "Why fake our deaths then inform Arashi we came back from the dead? *That* is what doesn't make sense to me."

Keishla took off her helmet as well to breathe easier. "What do you think it is?"

"I don't know…" Zenrot admitted. "Question is… where did the civilians evacuate to?"

Keishla couldn't think of anything. She simply stretched her arms and stood from the chair. "Well, we've eliminated most of our enemies. It has been quite easy, to be honest." She sounded confident. Zenrot gazed at her armor, looking at the parts melted thanks to the Clambers, then looked back at his armor.

"For now," Zenrot agreed sarcastically, "I'm very sure there's more waiting for us."

Keishla laughed lightly. "Why do you have to ruin the fun? We got in, we are halfway to Arashi's building. We're stronger than ever, they won't stand a chance!"

A harsh static noise sounded through their communicators, startling them both.

"Having fun, guys?" Zenrot immediately stood up. *That voice…!* It was the voice of a man, confident and cocky, that they hadn't heard for days.

"Frederick!" Zenrot shouted furiously. "How the hell did you get into our communication?"

"We use the same device, dumbass. Plus, you're kind of obvious for what frequency you'll choose."

"Listen, you son of a bitch!" Keishla interfered. "If we ever see each other again, your head is mine!"

"Why betray us? Why did you try to kill us?" Zenrot asked Freddy.

"You'll get your answer in time. But for now, focus on Arashi. Then we'll talk. Over and out."

After Freddy hung up, a voice sounded from the emergency broadcast everyone on Art Gun could hear.

"Zenrot Bellator and Keishla Monulen! Well done for coming this far!" It was Arashi speaking. "I must admit, both of you have gotten stronger. I didn't think you had all that energy and courage in you." Zenrot and Keishla put their helmets back on and stepped outside the restaurant, on guard for any threat. Arashi kept talking. "Unfortunately, this is what I was afraid of. Now I must take severe action against traitors like you. Just like I did with Major Ryan."

Keishla snapped her attention to Zenrot. He was clenching his fists, and she knew Zenrot felt angry and devastated.

"Listen, Dark Boy," she tried to coach Zenrot, "I know it's hard, but keep your focus. I need you sharp right now. Arashi wants to get us desperate and let our guard down. We will finish him, and those who follow him, for good."

"He just called us traitors… and said he considered Ryan a traitor… and for what?" He looked at Keishla, desperate and confused.

"I—I don't know…" Keishla said quietly, uncertain herself. "I don't know why Arashi tried to kill us."

"Now I want to end this…" Zenrot pulls out his sword, "I NEED ANSWERS!"

"We will get them." Keishla took out her knife bow, "just please keep your focus."

"While you guys have been busy," Arashi continued, "we've been working on a new project to deal with mutant terrorists. With this, you can see how strong you are against yourselves. Say hello to our new prototype." Zenrot and Keishla saw someone flying toward them, coming all the way from Arashi's building. "Meet the ACC." (Artificial Clone Combat).

The figure landed in front of them, cracking the ground with its weight. It was a giant robot with a body that looked very human, constructed with metal parts. The robot's face was covered by a metal mask. It stood straight and still, no sign of movement.

"Be on guard, probably a new enemy invented from the intel we recovered," Zenrot cautioned.

"Well, he hasn't moved at all. Probably scared of us, I mean it is two versus one."

"Like you said before, don't let your guard down," Zenrot answered back. "Besides, look around you. There is no one else but that thing. It must be pretty powerful."

"INITIATING SCANNING PROGRAM," the ACC said.

Zenrot and Keishla immediately went into a full defensive position. Red lights came out of the robot's eyes. They moved fast, pointing and scanning Zenrot from top to bottom. It immediately scanned across Keishla's body as well.

"Hey, you pervert! Like what you see? Get ready for the beating of a lifetime," she screamed furiously at the robot.

"SCANNING COMPLETE. INITIATE BATTLE FRE-QUENCY," the robot announced. Stretching its right arm, the ACC released a portion of energy. The energy formed into a sword in its right hand, while its left hand formed a revolver. It was imitating Zenrot's weapons. Around the robot energy daggers coalesced into existence, floating in the air the same as Keishla's.

Keishla looked at Zenrot with a poker face underneath the dark helmet, "So, he's our own action figure— like the two of us for the price of one?" Even in this tense situation she was speaking sarcastically.

"That might explain why they desperately wanted the intel from Sentry Run," Zenrot theorized. "They wanted to create their own mutant robots so they would obey their direct orders."

"Doesn't make sense. We followed their direct orders, always."

"We did… but maybe he thinks we can turn him down since we have our own free will." Zenrot walked forward, putting the sword over his shoulder. "They just want someone who won't question his orders. Arashi always preferred it that way."

"Fucking old man. I always had my doubts about the general."

Keishla, being confident, moved comfortably into a battle position. "Well, this should be fun. Hope you're ready, Dark Boy." She stepped ahead of Zenrot, releasing her daggers and taking the knife bow in her hands. Her daggers clashed with the ACC's daggers, and the robot swung with its sword from above. Keishla dodged by moving to the side. The sword passed a few inches to one side of her head and cut the tip of her ponytail off instead.

Keishla jumped back from the ACC, quickly spoke to Zenrot before she continued to engage the robot.

"Well, one thing's for sure, his clone weapons are quite amazing. I'll keep up close, you cover me!" She got in position to fight with her knife bow. The ACC banished the energy of its gun, reforming it into a shield. Keishla slashed with her knife bow rapidly, trying to maintain pressure on the robot, but the ACC protected itself with the shield. Unfortunately, Keishla got carried away. The robot pivoted and was bringing another attack from above with the sword; this time, one that Keishla couldn't dodge.

Zenrot rushed to help and jumped at the robot, kicking its arm away. The ACC moved back, and Zenrot fought with his sword in one hand and revolver in the other, alternating strikes. He broke the energy shield with several heavy blows from his blade, then quickly shot the upper arm, the chest, and one leg at the ACC while it was uncovered.

Zenrot tried to eliminate it with the sword, but the ACC caught it with its bare hand. Zenrot shot many times, however, the robot created the energy shield and blocked the incoming bullets. It lifted Zenrot and hurled him into the sky. The robot leapt into the air to follow. Zenrot noticed it was coming and they exchanged blows in midair until the robot landed a direct hit on Zenrot's face, hard enough to send him careening to the ground. Zenrot was thankful he was wearing a helmet.

The robot adjusted to land by stomping on top of the mutant. Zenrot yelled in pain. The robot was about to smash him in the face with his fist, but Keishla jumped at the robot and kicked it on the left side of its body, pushing it away. Keishla threw one of her daggers, stabbing it in the chest. She moved to Zenrot while the robot was unsteady.

"Are you all right?" She was desperately worried after watching the monstrous hits Zenrot had just taken. She pulled him up so he could stand.

Zenrot took off his helmet, spat blood from his mouth, then pulled the armor back on. "I'm fine, but this thing copies any weapons and energy. Who knows what else it can do?"

"No one is original these days," Keishla said sarcastically.

Their armor was scratched and sunken in many areas, but they rushed in to fight together at the same time. Zenrot jumped high, shooting his revolver at the robot. He hit the ACC with two energy bullets close to where a heart would be located. Keishla attacked the same area with her knife bow, only creating scratches into the metal.

The robot's weapon quickly banished, the ACC switched to a defensive position and waited for an opening against the mutants. With precise timing, the robot grabbed Keishla's face. It smashed her against the ground, forcing her to let go of the knife bow and unable to telekinetically control her daggers. The robot was trying to squish her head with its bare hands.

"Keishla!" Zenrot ran toward the ACC firing a volley of energy bullets with his revolver. The robot's daggers appeared and parried the incoming shots. Zenrot jumped with his sword, trying for a one-handed slash from above. The robot slid away, however, dragging Keishla along on the floor. The ACC was waiting for the perfect moment.

The robot swung to the side, and with its free arm, grabbed Zenrot by the neck. It choked him hard enough that he dropped his weapons. The robot was holding them both for a moment, then decided to eliminate Keishla first. It increased the pressure on her, crushing her helmet slowly and torturing her until her head was squashed.

Zenrot struggled, punching the robot's hand to break out, but the robot wasn't taking damage. Hearing the creaking of her helmet, Keishla drew the sword from her waist and tried to stab the robot's arm but couldn't see. The sword bounced off the arm; the iron was strong. Losing strength and feeling herself growing faint, Keishla threw the sword into the air, hoping Zenrot could do something with it. Her eyes fluttered shut; she was about to pass out completely.

Suffering from the choke, Zenrot saw the sword tumbling close through the air. He waited until it was within reach and grabbed it. Focused all his energy into the blade and, with all his available strength, sliced through the robot's arm. Zenrot fell to the ground and, desperate to put space between the machine, immediately delivered a powerful punch to its face. It was enough to knock the ACC away, freeing Keishla. Her helmet was all sunken and crumpled, and Zenrot panicked. He lifted her up by putting his arm on her back, then tore off her helmet and threw it away. He didn't even know if she was still conscious, or worse, alive. "Keishla! Are you all right?" Zenrot shouted as he shook her.

Keishla opened her eyes and looked at him, struggling to speak. "Do I look okay? I almost got smashed." She had pain in her voice.

Zenrot laughed, despite the severity of the situation, in genuine relief. "I'm glad your attitude is still intact." He helped steady her and both looked at the ACC, standing with one arm missing. Zenrot and Keishla were exhausted from fighting.

Keishla looked frustrated to Zenrot. "It's outmatching us! At this rate the metal freak will kill us if we don't do something fast. Any ideas?"

Zenrot looked at the robot, trying to find a weak spot to strike it down. Looking where he had cut the robot's arm, he saw something glowing blue coming from the hole. "It seems that it has a power core on the inside that keeps him running," Zenrot shouted, "if we destroy that, we might actually win this!"

"How the hell are we going to get close to that?" Keishla responded with frustration, pointing at the robot. "We fought him together and he almost killed us."

Zenrot thought of an approach to beat the robot and came up with a plan. "Here, take my gun, wait for my signal." He tossed her the revolver and ran to the ACC, alone.

"What the heck?" Keishla yelled, confused.

"Just follow my lead!"

The robot released a sword with its energy, blocking Zenrot's sword. Both were clashing the blades, the ACC fighted with a single hand and reacted very quickly. The robot revealed all the energy daggers and throwed them at Zenrot to stab him. Zenrot jumped high, dodging the daggers, put the sword on his back and fell near the robot to fight it hand to hand. The robot swung its sword sideways, but Zenrot slid on his knees, leaning back to dodge the sword. It passed right in front of his face.

Zenrot quickly uppercut the ACC right between the legs, bending the metal. He punched the robot's only hand to interrupt its ability to use the sword, and proceeded to punch in the chest several times. Keeping it off balance, he jumped into a roundhouse kick, striking the robot in the face with his heel and knocking it to the ground.

Zenrot jumped on the robot and tried to open its chest with his bare hands. The aura of dark energy showed around his hands as Zenrot drew on all his strength. He haltingly tore open the chest, bending the iron covering inside and revealing the electronics and power core. The ACC caught Zenrot with a punch that was hard enough to knock him away.

Zenrot quickly recovered and rushed the robot while it was still getting up. He went behind and held it tight with his arms, looking at Keishla.

"Now's your chance, shoot it!" he yelled.

Keishla aimed at the robot's power core with Zenrot's revolver, focusing all her energy to blast straight in its core. However, something was holding her back.

"What are you waiting for? Shoot the gun!" Zenrot shouted, struggling to hold the robot in position.

"What about you? You may blow up with it!"

"Now is not the time, shoot this thing!"

Keishla was afraid to shoot, knowing Zenrot was behind the robot and could die. Time was passing, and the ACC was forming new daggers with its energy. Zenrot was scared the robot would recover its weapons, he needed Keishla to take the shot. Zenrot had an idea that might regret the decision later.

"KEISHLA! FOR ONCE IN YOUR LIFE, STOP BEING A BITCH AND TAKE AN ORDER! SHOOT, DAMN IT!"

"What did you just say to me? You're dead!" That snapped her out. Finding motivation in her anger, Keishla charged the gun with all the energy she could and released the shot. A yellow beam of energy impact the robot's core, it overcharged and blowed it into pieces. Zenrot was pushed away and crashed against a wall before bouncing to the floor. Keishla ran straight to check on Zenrot, reaching him and dropping to her knees next to him.

"Hey idiot, you still alive?" Zenrot lifted his hand to his face, took off the helmet, and threw it away to breathe better.

"I'm all right," he said lightly. "About time you took the shot." Zenrot chuckled as Keishla got angry, punching him in the chest and cussing him out. Even if Zenrot had to get on Keishla's nerves for her to make a move, and it had almost cost him his life, she was just glad he made it through alive. Keishla leaned back on the ground feeling relieved.

"Glad that's over," she said calmly.

Zenrot slowly stood up, retrieving his revolver and putting it inside his holster. He turned his head, looking at Arashi's building. "Don't relax just yet, the worst is yet to come."

"Ugh… can't this day end?" Keishla's calm fluidly turned into irritation.

Zenrot grabbed Keishla's hand to help her stand up. Keishla returned her daggers to her backpack with her telekinesis, reseated the sword in her scabbard, and held the knife bow in one hand. Both walked toward Art Gun's main building, getting closer to the inevitable confrontation with Arashi. They were getting close when Zenrot nudged Keishla, pointing out someone standing in their way in front of the headquarters building. Looking closely, they recognized who it was.

"Frederick."

Freddy was standing with his arms crossed and his scythe on his back. Zenrot has his hand on the butt of his revolver, ready to draw it if needed. Keishla was holding her fists tight, trying not to engage and beat the shit out of Freddy. Both stared with a heated mix of caution and anger, while Freddy, on the other side, seemed relaxed. He looked confident, smiling in a sinister way. Surprisingly, he started applauding.

"My, my… You really made it this far. I'm so proud of you guys."

"I suppose you won't let us through?" Zenrot said flatly.

Keishla was getting more furious by the second while looking at Freddy. "We have some questions for Arashi, then we'll deal with you! Either get out of our way… or I will cut off your head and take it as a trophy when we get out of here."

Freddy smoothly pulled the scythe from his back, and pointed the weapon at them. "Please… is that a way to treat a friend? Besides, you're still alive because I let you both live. I knew you guys would take care of anyone in your way."

Keishla gasped because what Zenrot had guessed was true—Freddy had let them get away back in Rasenof.

"Honestly," Freddy continued speaking, "I didn't expect you to destroy half of Art Gun's base. Besides…" His smile faded away. "I was waiting for this moment, the big finale!" he shouted in anger.

"What the hell is he talking about?" Keishla said, turning her head and momentarily locking eyes with Zenrot.

"I don't know, but I think we're about to find out."

CHAPTER
TWELVE

There was no one left around Art Gun's base. Only Zenrot, Keishla, and Freddy were on the field. The three of them faced each other. If Freddy was guarding the building, Arashi must have been hiding in his office.

"Frederick." Zenrot heard a voice coming from a distant communicator. Freddy puts a finger on his ear. *"My scanners indicate Zenrot and Keishla are standing right in front of you. Eliminate them."*

"Calm down, old man. They won't get past me. Give me a few minutes, will ya?" Freddy said while pacing.

"We must eliminate the threat immediately!"

"Yeah, yeah… I heard you." Freddy gazed with a smirk at Zenrot and Keishla. "Before we get to the main event…" he shut off his communication with Arashi. "I'm sure you guys have many questions," Zenrot and Keishla looked at each other, confused and wondering if this was a trick or if he was actually serious, "so go on, ask away. What do you want to know?"

"Just like that?" Zenrot asked with an eyebrow raised.

"Well, as a reward for getting this far, sure. Try to be quick, I have work to do."

"The hell do you have to do?" Keishla shouted. Zenrot raised his hand as a sign to calm herself.

"Where are the civilians?" Zenrot asked. Freddy seemed surprised that was his first question.

"Most people were evacuated," Freddy answered. "After our incident in Rasenof, Arashi wanted to move the base. It was clear that Sentry Run was finally defeated. We cleaned most cities of their troops, and their main headquarters was no longer operating. So it's safe to say we can start giving a home to the civilians."

"Then why are you guys still here?" Zenrot asked. "And why kill us? After everything we did for Art Gun and the people." Zenrot remembered what Arashi had said in the broadcast: he and Keishla were considered traitors.

"We're here to make sure no trace is left that you two ever existed." Freddy rolls his eyes as an expression that he judged it a stupid decision, Zenrot and Keishla felt a mix of shock, anger, and insult. "Arashi is calling you a traitor right now as an excuse since you didn't die according to his plan." Freddy exhaled a long breath. "According to the bald guy, he wanted to form an army of mutants to show the world that humans and mutants can bond together, blah, blah, blah… you get the idea." Freddy spoke with a mocking tone, "However, he got frightened. His thoughts were eating him alive."

"About what exactly?" Zenrot asked.

"About the possibility of the mutants deciding to betray Art Gun."

"What do you mean by that?" Keishla intervene.

"Simple. Since you and Zenrot have gotten stronger, it's only a matter of time before you are powerful enough to take out a huge population—like the rumors about the mutant who wiped out a whole city, or the other one killing hundreds of people at the circus show. People are glad we defeated Sentry Run, but they're afraid that mutants are the only reason we won." Freddy glanced up at Arashi's building. "They spoke to Arashi about their safety. How are they going to live peacefully when a mutant could go sideways and decide to embrace evil. Who is going to stop them?" He turned to smoke, then appeared right between Zenrot and Keishla, laying his arms over their shoulders. "I mean, let's face it. Since we fought together, no one has stood a chance against us."

Keishla freed herself and swung her arm to hit Freddy but he turned into smoke once again. He returned to his original form right in front of Zenrot and Keishla.

"So, Arashi started to give it some thought. At first he wasn't happy with the idea, but watching how the MSF fought… made it clear the people were speaking the truth. So he came up with a plan. Arashi wanted to get all the intel from Sentry Run since they have the advanced technology to defeat a mutant, however, he didn't want the MSF to have any information about it."

"That's why we were sent alone on the mission… and denied our petition for reinforcements…" Zenrot spoke softly.

Freddy snapped his fingers, pointing at Zenrot. "Now you're getting the idea."

"It still doesn't make sense at all!" Zenrot shouted angrily. "We did everything Art Gun asked us to do. Served by their side. Why would they ever think we'll go against them after everything we've been through?"

Freddy raised his arms as if he was also questioning the situation.

"Beats me. All I know is that Arashi wants humans without special abilities strong enough to fight an actual mutant, or even twice stronger." Freddy then rolled his eyes, looking away. "Also, according to Arashi, you specifically needed to be eliminated, Zenrot, because you're growing too attached to people. That could lead us to a wrong path." Freddy then turned his eyes on Keishla. "And you… they wanted you eliminated because you are a reckless person, giving a hard time to the people who treated your wounds in the medical clinic."

"You know those assholes were treating me awful!" Keishla screamed in anger. "Instead of healing me, they treated me worse. Hurting a few of my wounds on purpose—just because I was a mutant! Sure, I had the intention to cut their heads off, but never hurt a single fucker! Because I knew they'll call Arashi to 'do something about me.'"

"Their words. Not mine."

"What about Astred?" Zenrot asked. "Why did Art Gun decide to kill him? He worked with them far longer than us."

"Because he's too smart." Zenrot and Keishla looked at him in confusion. "To rephrase it, Astred was going to find out Art Gun's plan sooner or later. Obviously, he wasn't going to allow it. Especially killing you guys. Honestly, I was surprised he was killed by the robots back at Sentry Run's headquarters. He was the only person I was worried on facing."

"You son of a—"

"Wait a second!" Keishla shouted, interrupting Zenrot. "If they wanted us dead back in Sentry Run's headquarters… how come they didn't decide to kill you?"

"Because I had proven to be a worthy mutant."

"More like prove to be a dick," Keishla hissed.

"What about Major Ryan? What did Arashi do to him?" Zenrot raised his voice, demanding. "What did Arashi do to him?" he asked again.

"I think you know what he did," Freddy said quietly. "Just to be clear, I wasn't aware of that. I'm sorry."

"Yet you still served him?" Zenrot screamed in fury.

"Please," Freddy said confidently, "I could give a damn about Arashi's decisions."

"Then why the hell did you try to kill us? What is your purpose? I thought we were your friends!" Keishla was heartbroken after being together as a team for so long.

Freddy laughed so hard he could barely breathe. "We were a squad, partners who worked together. That is all."

"You don't believe in that shit!" Keishla replied, pain ringing clear through her voice.

"Believe what you want to believe. Now, if I wanted you dead, I would have done it back in Rasenof Forest. You two were underwater in the waterfall holding your breath until I left. I know because you left one of your daggers on the floor and you stopped focusing. The dagger twitched from your telekinesis. I let you guys live so you could do me a favor."

"And what would that be?" Zenrot asked.

"To bring Art Gun to its knees!" Freddy shouted in anger. His hair ignited in a burst of fire. Zenrot and Keishla held tight to their weapons in case they needed to attack. "You see, back when Zenrot was working on his gun with Mojo, I found a folder with my name stamped on the top of his desk. It was strange, I've never worked with the scientist guy, so I kind of took it to see what it was. Turns out I'm not a living being with his own free will… I was created from a damned human corpse!" Zenrot and Keishla opened their eyes wide. The last point Freddy made definitely got their attention. "They picked a body who died exploring forbidden areas and created their own mutant—me! Art Gun made me fight for them! Designed to kill under their command, selling the world lies that they rescued me with their efforts. Giving me fake memories which I even find it hard to remember! This company is supposed to defend the mutants, not to fucking use us as they please."

Freddy was getting angrier and angrier, his flaming hair increasing in intensity. They could feel the heat from where they stood. "What other tricks do they have up their sleeves? What other excuse will they use to protect their pride as saving the different? They only care about their title—nothing more!"

"I am sorry that you were created, I really am…" Zenrot said softly, trying to talk Freddy out of his anger. "But why turn your back on us? We could've been there for you to figure this out together."

"There's nothing to figure out. Besides, the file says I was created to be a killing machine. So let's go with what it says on the paper. I will not let you two get in my way."

Zenrot concluded that there was no way to talk Freddy out of it anymore. He had gone mad, his anger and frustration clouded his thoughts. He had a giant smile on his face; Zenrot and Keishla watched how Freddy was a mutant heading down to an evil path. He took out the scythe, ready to fight.

Keishla looked at him with a poker face and said, "it's funny with all the shit you told us and you still follow orders. What makes you think he won't kill you once you're no use to him? Not to mention, you told his secret to us."

Freddy raised his left arm, releasing a massive surge of fire energy. Zenrot and Keishla stood in position, but Freddy turned his face toward Arashi's building.

"Oh, him?" He turned his eyes to Zenrot. "Arashi is in his office." Freddy's face grew enlightened, "Since he killed Ryan, allow me to give you a gift for all the trouble." Freddy turned his communication back to Arashi back on. "Hey, boss!"

"Frederick!" Arashi screamed in anger. *"Quit fooling around and eliminate Zenrot and Keishla!"*

"Relax, this will be easy. They might want to turn on their device to hear this." Freddy said. "I will proceed to finish them off, but I'm afraid… you won't get to see it happen."

"WHAT? WHAT THE HELL DO YOU MEAN BY THAT?"

"You know exactly what it means… goodbye, old man."

Freddy pulled back his arm, his left hand filled with flame, then threw the fire at the entrance door of the building. Flames melted the door and burned across the first floor. Explosions occurred within from the intensity of the flames. Windows broke and flames flared out and up as the inferno kept rising, consuming floor after floor.

"WHAT ARE YOU DOING!" Arashi yelled in the communicator. *"STOP THIS INSTANT! YOU WILL BE HUNTED JUST LIKE ZENROT AND KEISHLA!"*

"I look forward to it."

The flames reached the final floor.

"AAAAGHHH! YOU SON OF A—" Static came across everyone's radios. Zenrot and Keishla tossed theirs away at the intense static. Both watched as the building fell into the flame. People were falling from the window as they burned. Arashi and everyone else inside were gone.

"Well, that takes care of everything." Freddy tossed his radio away. "I don't think anyone will come out after that." He turned around, facing Zenrot and Keishla with a smirk. "Now… where were we?"

Zenrot and Keishla were in shock, feeling almost traumatized. Both had their mouths open in awe at how fast Freddy blew up the building like it was nothing.

"Well damn…" Keishla said, "he took that building down in seconds!"

"We have to be extremely careful with him," Zenrot said seriously. He was frightened because of how powerful Freddy was. "Last time he wasn't trying to kill us, but now is a different story."

"Yeah… two or three hits and we can kiss our ass goodbye."

"Probably one energy blast from him… if he goes serious," Zenrot answered with sarcasm.

Freddy started getting impatient. "Come on guys," Freddy shouted, "as much as I love our reunion, I have a busy schedule eliminating every living being to attend to."

"Well, the firecracker is needy…" Keishla said with her eyes rolling to Zenrot, "Any plans?"

He thought for a quick second, "Engage close combat, I'll cover your back."

Keishla looks at him seriously. "Why am I always in close combat?"

"Because you like it personal."

"Fair enough, you ready?" Keishla looked at Zenrot and with her knife bow in hand.

Zenrot took out his revolver with one hand and the sword in the other. "Oh, I'm ready."

"Then let's—" Keishla was blown away and impacted against a building. Part of the building fell on top of her. Freddy had shot her with a fire blast from his hand. She stood up quickly, removing the debris on top of her, looking very angry. "You bitch!"

Keishla immediately sprinted towards Freddy with her knife bow. Getting close, she swung it at about a forty-five-degree angle. Freddy blocked it with his scythe using only one hand. He pushed her away with a kick and rushed to attack. While the blades clashed, parrying one another, Freddy had an opening and charged a fire energy with his other hand.

Zenrot took him by surprise, kicking Freddy's hand to blow his energy away. Freddy turned into smoke, trying to escape. He regained his original form miles away, but Keishla was already close. They continued fighting. Zenrot used his revolver, charging it with enough energy then aiming at Freddy and opening fire. While Freddy was fighting Keishla, he used his free hand and threw fire around his back to protect himself from

Zenrot's bullets. Using the revolver wouldn't work. Zenrot ran to close the distance to Freddy and fought up close.

Noticing he was getting close, Freddy dodged Keishla's attack. He quickly returned the scythe to his back and punched Keishla twice in the face, hard enough to knock her down. Freddy ran away, but Zenrot closed and swung with his sword. Freddy blocked with the scythe.

Zenrot delivered a two-handed slash with his sword, but Freddy walked backwards and dodged, using the scythe to push the sword inches away. He turned the staff around, putting the knife-edge of the scythe upside down. Freddy tried to hit Zenrot down and slice him to the top of his torso, but Zenrot reacted and jumped back. As Freddy swung the scythe it lit on fire, a fire which then shot from the blade in the shape of a half-moon. Zenrot blocked the fire with his sword and weathered the strong impact, however, Freddy was nowhere to be seen.

"Over here," Freddy whispered. Zenrot turned around and Freddy attacked at maximum speed with a combination of kicks. The last kick hit Zenrot's chest, followed by a swing of the scythe to slice Zenrot in half. Keishla's daggers got in the way and blocked it. Her knife bow was returned to her backpack. She drew her sword from her scabbard, jumped very high into the air, and fell to stab Freddy from above.

Keishla missed, stabbing her blade into the ground. She and Zenrot rushed together and attacked Freddy at the same time, combining their techniques. Both kept to close combat, but his reflexes were amazing. He dodged every attack, blocked some strikes with his scythe, and spread fire around to protect himself. Freddy was making absolutely sure he was not being touched.

Zenrot and Keishla jumped away from Freddy. Zenrot took out his revolver and shot multiple energy bullets, but the fire burned them away as well. He charged his revolver with immense amounts of dark energy and shot Freddy. A giant wall of fire appeared in front of him as a shield, consuming the entire energy bullet.

"This is not good," Keishla said nervously.

"Never forget, his energy comes naturally and protects him from incoming attacks, so before we can do significant damage upon him, we either have to make Freddy lower his energy or catch him by surprise." Zenrot quoted to have in mind while they fought. Freddy held the scythe with both hands, stretching his arms up and starting to circle around, creating a giant fireball. It was as big as a five-story building.

Zenrot and Keishla looked up, both shocked and impressed at how much energy he was using.

Keishla's mouth dropped open. "Oh mother—"

"This fight will be more difficult…" Zenrot interrupted.

"All right guys, let's see you figure out this one!" Freddy screamed furiously. He threw the fireball, which fell slowly towards them. Zenrot charged his revolver with a huge amount of energy and shot the fireball, making a huge explosion. Buildings crumbled into pieces and ash. Keishla rushed to Freddy, putting her sword in her scabbard, and jumped high while drawing her knife bow. While in the air, she started shooting energy arrows.

While she was fighting Freddy, Zenrot was thinking of something big: how to inflict actual damage. He had an idea to use the rocket launcher against Freddy, in the same way as he had used it against the army. He ran around the field of dead soldiers and, after a minute of searching, finally found one with a rocket. Zenrot moved to a very long-range position to employ the same technique. He dropped to his knees, aiming the rocket launcher at where Freddy and Keishla were located and started charging his energy.

Keishla was still fighting Freddy. Both were moving with intensity. She used her daggers with her telekinesis to try and hit Freddy, but he used the pressure of his fire and pushed them back. She walked backwards with her bow, shooting energy arrows, but Freddy had his fire floating around protecting him. Unexpectedly, he dashed close enough for an attack with his scythe from above. Keishla blocked with the knife of her bow, feeling the heat of the fire.

"Keishla! Get out of there now!" Zenrot screamed. Keishla took a quick look at Zenrot and saw what he had planned. Zenrot finished charging the revolver. Freddy was about to attack with his scythe again, so she dodged by moving to the side and quickly going to his back. She grabbed the back of his head and pushed him to the ground. Her hands burned as she touched Freddy. After knocking him over, Keishla immediately ran to Zenrot's direction.

Zenrot took the shot with the rocket launcher, then shot its explosive with his revolver. A huge energy blast passed Keishla, and a few seconds later she heard the explosion. She reached Zenrot and took a closer look at where Freddy had been standing. It was a direct hit.

"Did we get him?" Keishla asked, breathing hard from exhaustion.

"I don't know," Zenrot said, exhausted as well. He put the rocket launcher on the ground. Watching the smoke fading away, they saw neon orange lines glowing in the distance and wondered what it could be. When the smoke is gone, Freddy is still standing. He was wearing the same armor as Zenrot and Keishla.

"Impossible…" Zenrot said weakly.

Freddy was laughing as he walked slowly to them. "You guys didn't think I wasn't prepared, did you?"

"When the fuck did he get a pauldron?" Keishla said in frustration.

"You left one in the helicopter, dumbass. I must admit, it's a bit uncomfortable fighting wearing this." Freddy yanked off his helmet. "Ahh… much better." He grabbed the scythe while energy spiraling off his hand around its shaft.

Keishla looked at Zenrot nervously. "Now what's he up to?"

"I don't know! Stay alert."

Freddy dropped a small bit of blood from his lips and cleaned it with his finger. "You two are pretty strong. I can see why the soldiers and robots failed to kill you. But I got something better for you. How about I bring a new army?" He raised his scythe. Fire was coming out of the blade. "And drag you both straight to hell!" Freddy hit the ground with the staff of the scythe. The fire flew from the blade in lines, arching through the air to the many dead bodies scattered around the battlefield. People slowly stood, their skin burnt and some showing their skeletons. On their forehead there was a symbol of fire, a mark that identified they were being controlled. Hundreds of them gathered to attack.

Freddy pointed with his scythe to where Zenrot and Keishla were standing. "Revenants of flame, kill them!" Freddy's army moved slowly as they built speed to run towards them. The creatures left trails of fire as they ran.

Meanwhile, Zenrot and Keishla were watching Freddy's army getting closer to them. They had a few minutes until they arrived, so Keishla sat on the ground to rest for a few seconds. Zenrot got on his knees, breathing heavily.

"Ignoring the obvious situation… how are you feeling?" He tried to phrase it in a way which prevented Keishla from giving a sarcastic answer. He was worried about what was going to happen when they started fighting again. His energy was almost drained.

Keishla had all her daggers on the floor next to her in case she had to engage from afar. Her legs were crossed, sitting on the ground still breathing hard.

"Well… tired as hell, to be honest. Fighting an entire upgraded army of Art Gun, a mutant robot that can copy our weapons and abilities, dealing with this guy, and now we must face a new army on fire that is even creepier than Mojo. I'm exhausted."

Zenrot struggled to stand up for how tired he was. He looked straight forward to the army. "There's not much to be discussed then. If we die here, let us take out as many as we can and do our best to finish Freddy." He spoke with a firm voice. "If anything goes wrong, I will use the rest of my energy to create a strong blast to wipe this whole place. Even if it takes my life. If they don't die, it should give you enough time to make a run for it. So be ready t—"

"You're an imbecile, you know that?" she said the words holding venom but her tone soft. Zenrot gasped and looked at her with surprise. She stood up and picked up her knife bow. Her daggers floated as she also looked toward the upcoming army. "If you think I'm going to let you die alone, you're wrong. We came this far together. If we fight as a team, we die as a team… You hear me? Don't ever forget that!" Keishla charged a big energy arrow, aimed it up, and released the shot. The arrow climbed, then arced down to the incoming army. It blew apart on impact, taking at least fifteen fire revenants down. "I said, 'did you hear me?'" she yelled. Zenrot just smiled at her and nodded in agreement. "Besides," she continued talking as she kept shooting arrows, "I'm going to be the one who's going to cut your head off your neck if we ever become enemies."

"Roger that… Let's go!" Zenrot answered, and chuckled.

The army would reach them any moment, and Freddy was behind the crew, relaxed. Having such confidence in his malicious plans. "Come at me, guys! I'll turn you both into ash!"

CHAPTER THIRTEEN

In a warehouse, very far from the battle between Zenrot, Keishla, and Frederick, was a base hidden with a broad variety of mechanical parts and tools which would belong in an engineering lab. An alarm was sounding, reacting directly to Freddy's intense energy. Something inside the lab began to respond.

"IT SEEMS FREDERICK CROSSVELT HAS MADE HIS CHOICE… ACTIVATING ALL SYSTEMS."

CHAPTER FOURTEEN

The army reached Zenrot and Keishla. Both fought the fire Revenants while keeping their distance. Keishla shot with her bow and Zenrot with his revolver. Some of the fire Revenants exploded when hit; some kept moving slowly forward. The most effective way to kill the fire Revenants was shooting their heads. Zenrot fired on every one he could and, if they got too close, used his sword to push them to a distance safe. As he was fighting with caution, one of them jumped Zenrot from the back. Others started to follow. Thirteen managed to pile on top of him, forcing Zenrot to his knees and burning his armor with their bodies. Zenrot He lurched to his feet and, with all his strength, swung around to shake them off. One still clung on top of his back, so he lifted his arm up, grabbed it by the neck, and pulled. He tossed the Revenant against the floor and ended it with his sword by stabbing the creature through the head.

One Revenant managed to get close and hit her by surprise. She sliced it through the waist with her knife bow. Many enemies were coming from different directions. Keishla used her daggers with her telekinesis and stabbed them by passing the knife through their heads. She killed all the close fire Revenants and saw another group from afar. She picked the smallest dagger and moved it like a boomerang, whirling it in a deadly arc which sliced their heads in rapid succession.

Frederick smashed the ground with his energy, cracking the surrounding earth. He started lifting a giant boulder full of fire big enough to squish everyone. His body started releasing energy and, with his bare fists, he pushed the boulder toward Zenrot and Keishla. They saw the giant boulder rolling their way, passing over Revenants on its way. Keishla braced herself, taking a position ready to face the giant boulder. Zenrot glanced over and could see her shaking in exhaustion; he knew she was not capable of stopping something that big. Zenrot walked forward and stood in front of her.

"Hold it, you won't make it if you try to stop it," Zenrot said.

"Well, do you have a better plan?"

"Yeah, but it will use a lot of my energy, so get ready to defend," Zenrot answered. He put his sword into its scabbard and his gun in his holster. Focusing his energy on his hands, Zenrot felt pain throughout his body but, with strength and effort, mustered enough energy to stop it.

Despite burning his fingers, Zenrot reversed its momentum. He held the boulder up with one hand and punched it hard with the other. The massive burning stone crumbled into pieces. After it was destroyed, he fell to his knees, exhausted. A couple of the Revenants ran to Zenrot, jumping on him while he was down.

Keishla stepped in and defended Zenrot while he recovered; prevented anyone from touching him and killed them.

Zenrot and Keishla felt another tremble. Another giant, flaming boulder was approaching.

"Talk about overkill…" Keishla said, agitation and frustration commingled in her tone.

Zenrot stood up, shaking his head. "I won't be able to stop the second one in time, fall back!"

Both made a run for it and more Revenants were rising from the ground. Keishla took point, clearing the path for Zenrot with her knife bow. Those Revenants coming from the ground caught energy arrows, and her telekinetically propelled daggers killed those already standing. Those she missed fell courtesy of Zenrot's revolver. Feeling marginally recovered, Zenrot stopped running. Keishla noticed he wasn't close, having stopped a few feet away. He was waiting for the boulder to get closer, then, a few seconds later, Zenrot jumped. He used his legs to push it and himself away at the same time. He shot it with a massive energy bullet from his revolver, blowing it away.

More fire Revenants were coming. Zenrot and Keishla were almost laying down, exhausted by fighting and running all day. They had no choice but to fight for their lives if they wanted to win. Freddy was staying just far enough away, summoning the army Zenrot and Keishla kept fighting over and over. They seemed inexhaustible.

"Dark Boy!" Keishla screamed. "We can't keep this up much longer. Any new plan you can suggest?"

"None! The best we can do is keep holding our ground until

Freddy can't summon more of his army," Zenrot replied, agitated and shooting at Revenants.

"That's not going to happen—there's too many of them!" Keishla responded back. She laid down for a second to breathe and a Revenant jumped on her, pushing her to the ground. She was unable to focus to use her energy while trying to get the Revenant off of her. More of them jumped on Keishla and then there were too many holding her back.

Zenrot looked back and saw she was in trouble. On his way to help her, another group of Revenants jumped him. Surprised, Zenrot was pushed to the ground. Both mutants struggled to get out, feeling the burn from the Revenants across their bodies. Their armor was slowly melting.

I guess this is our fate... Those were Zenrot's thoughts.

PAM, PAM, PAM. Zenrot and Keishla heard gunshots. The Revenants stopped moving, each having been shot in their head. They both immediately took to their feet, panicked.

"The fuck happened?" Keishla yelled, confused at what could have just saved them at the last second. A squad of soldiers moved into view, approaching. Both could see their uniforms; on their chests they wore Art Gun's logo. On their right arms were the colors denoting their ranks. "And who the hell are you guys?" she asked. One soldier stepped forward and saluted, snapping his arm up and to the front of his forehead.

"Captain Randell of the shadow squad reporting for duty, madam."

"You guys sure have guts to stand in front of us after what happened today," Zenrot angrily said through gritted teeth. He was mad because he didn't trust their intentions; everyone from Art Gun thus far tried to kill him and Keishla.

"We're here to repay our debt to you, sir." Randell turned halfway to the side and stretched his arm out to introduce his team, five other men from the shadow squad. Their names were Daniel, John, Kevin, Robert J., and Arnold. "Besides," he said, looking straight back to Zenrot. "We are also here to avenge Major Ryan's death."

Zenrot was shocked at the mention of Ryan's name. He lifted his sword, pointing it at the soldiers. "What the hell do you know about him? He was killed by Arashi!" he screamed angrily at Randell.

"He used to be the captain of our team. *Our* captain. He retired when his son died in battle and promoted me to captain."

"Wait, his son… was from the shadow squad?" Zenrot asked. Randell nodded in confirmation.

"After that, Ryan decided to train new recruits to make good soldiers. When you came in, he was not pleased about training only a single mutant, but he saw something in you and wanted you to be the best soldier. I'm sure he had his reasons. We couldn't kill someone who was important to our former captain. Also, we didn't know that Arashi had murdered him. So we decided to hide until the time was right, even if we had orders to kill you both."

Freddy saw the squad had saved Zenrot and Keishla from afar. He chuckled. "Well, reinforcements, I see." The statement was as much a threat as an observation. "Let me give you all a proper welcome." He released fire from his scythe, sending it to more dead bodies. An even larger army of fire Revenants rose.

Zenrot, Keishla, and the shadow squad were getting ready for battle.

"So, what's the status?" Randell asked.

"Oh you know, playing around…" Keishla answered with her sarcastic, aggressive tone. "He's fucking kicking our asses, that's the situation!"

"Well, we'll have to kick *his* harder, then," Randell responded with confidence.

Zenrot wasn't convinced he could work alongside a squad of Art Gun, but he needed all the help he could get at this point. He looked at them with threatening eyes. "No offense, but the reason I haven't killed you guys right now is because you aided us with those fire Revenants. But I warn you, if you try anything funny against us… YOU. WILL. DIE!"

Daniel chuckled nervously, but John didn't look surprised.

"Don't worry, we already know that," Daniel assured.

"I told you guys he was going to get all mad," Kevin added.

John was laughing. "You guys owe me lunch later."

Randell, rifle in his hand, stood at attention, formal and rigid. "We would rather die for what is right than double cross you, sir!" He spoke as clearly and bravely as ever, with no doubt behind his words.

Keishla was happy with what Randell said. Feeling motivated, she stood up with her knife bow in her hands and her daggers floating in the air around her. She stomped the ground, feeling courage and confidence in herself.

"That's the spirit! Let's get this over with!" she said to the shadow squad then rushed to the Revenants and fight.

Zenrot didn't feel comfortable fighting alongside the squad, but if Keishla trusted them, he would as well. He sprinted to join Keishla in the fight against the Revenants. The shadow squad got their rifles ready, standing in a defensive position and keeping a lookout for any surprises. Revenants got close to Zenrot and Keishla, many of them coming from different directions.

"Enemy on site! Watch your back!" Randell shouted at his team. Danny and Kevin started shooting the enemy as they tactically moved forward to defend Zenrot. A few Revenants rans toward the shadow squad and attacked, but John and Arnold stood in front of the squad pushing the enemy back with shields, almost like the Spartan had. While John and Arnold kept them busy, Robert J. flanked the Revenants and finished them off with his shotgun, executing each one with a Remington Model 1100. Randell and his squad fought strategically; they were calm and effective even in this unusual situation, eliminating every fire Revenant which moved into range.

Keishla ran to Zenrot. "Shit, there is no end to them!"

"Cut the master's head off and they will all die," Zenrot responded.

"Heh. Copy that."

"I'll provide cover in case any of them start following you… Go!"

Keishla focused on her speed, moving fast enough across the battlefield to pass the whole army on her way to reach Frederick; to fight him one on one. Zenrot stayed on guard, fighting alongside the shadow squad. More Revenants tried to attack Zenrot, but he used his sword to swing through his enemies, cutting them down one after another. If one showed signs it was about to explode, he aimed with his revolver and blasted it away to prevent the explosion. Revenants circled around, trying to ambush Zenrot, but the squad had his back covered from every angle. Danny and Kevin killed the enemies at range with a Colt CAR-15 Commando while John and Arnold tried to round them up with their shields. They signaled Robert J. to throw a hand grenade and, after an accurate throw, blew up about twenty Revenants. Daniel, John, Robert J, Kevin, and Arnold all got excited when they blew the Revenants away.

"Oh, hell yeah!" Daniel screamed in joy.

"We're the best right now!" John followed up, continuing their conversation.

"Don't let your guard down boys, we still got work to do," Randell said seriously. In the middle of their conversation, an additional thirty Revenants came from the ground and ambushed the squad. Zenrot noticed they were in trouble and unloaded several shots at the Revenants. He finished the group off with four blasts of energy.

"Next time I won't save you all, so be on guard," Zenrot angrily warned before moving away to fight more Revenants.

***

Meanwhile, on the other side of the battlefield, Keishla was looking at him with a face of rage and the desire to slash his throat. Freddy had a smile on his face, pleased to kill her.

"Well then, show me what you got," he said greedily. Keishla saved her knife bow and the daggers on her backpack, except for one. She held one dagger and drew her sword out from her scabbard with the other hand. Looking for a personal fight, she sprinted to Freddy and swung with the blades from every direction, striking at his stomach, arms, and face… anywhere she could hit.

Freddy blocked every attack with the staff of the scythe. Keishla swung big with the sword and Freddy parried the attack using the blade of his scythe, then pushed her sword away. Keishla slashed with the dagger in her other hand. Freddy freed one hand from the scythe and caught Keishla's hand, crushing it into the handle of her own weapon until the pain forced her to let go of the dagger. When it dropped, he quickly stabbed his scythe against the floor and punched her in the face, knocking her to the ground.

"You know what your problem is, Keishla?" Freddy lectured. Keishla climbed back to her feet to hit him back, but he saw the move coming and kicked her in the ankle, forcing her to knee at the ground. He punched her again in the face. "The problem is that you always get desperate when you fight. You never focus, and that's why I've always been superior to you."

"It's funny," Keishla said as she spat blood from her mouth, "cause you hit like a bitch." Freddy lost his composure and punched her in the face hard enough to make Keishla dizzy. Still on her knees, she held her head with both hands trying to focus. Freddy walked around, standing behind her. Grabbing Keishla's hair, he pulled hard, forcing her to stand.

Freddy got close to her ear. "Pathetic," he whispered before kicking her in the back. She fell a few feet away, lying on the ground.

Keishla was thinking about her past, a time when she was training with Freddy way before Zenrot had joined the team. She remembered fighting hand to hand, when neither could use their abilities and she had never managed to defeat him. Remembering their last training fight, Keishla had been in a similar position: on the ground and looking up, staring at a face full of disappointment. Freddy only ever saw her as a partner so fragile. She remembered Freddy talking down to her then, too.

"If you wish to get better, you must worry about your own survival. Not for anyone else. If you think about the good of others besides yourself, you won't be alive for much longer."

Keishla pushed up to her feet, legs shaking, and turned to face Freddy. "You're right about one thing—that you said in the past…" she could hear herself babbling, and Freddy looked at her standing with something resembling actual concern. "Caring for other people, other than myself won't get me anywhere… all because I worried for the wrong person…" She thought about all the moments she'd shared with Astred, and how he had cared and protected her from everyone—even from Art Gun. She also thought of Zenrot, and how they had been fighting together to stay alive and protecting one another. The thought that he could've died if it wasn't for her, then it's reciprocal: they helped each other.

"Now I have someone fighting alongside me—besides my own ego-happy self," Keishla continued, "Unlike you, who wants to wipe everyone out in anger. You have lost yourself to madness and what you're doing is wrong. We will stop you! Even if it means for me to die here!" Keishla was standing straight with her hands down and fists tight, despite the sweat and blood running down her forehead, bruises all over her face, or mostly damaged and sunken armor.

Freddy was barely even touched, with only a few scratches to his face and his armor almost like new. He chuckled, "Very well," and tilted his head down, "after all, it's your funeral." He lifted his face up, surprised to see Keishla only inches away and swinging a fist to his face. Freddy dashed back and raised his arms to cover his face. Keishla took the opportunity and rained punches from his stomach to his chest.

Freddy grabbed her right hand and twisted it up with his left. Pulling her close, Freddy was about to hit her with his right hand when Keishla headbutted him hard enough for him to momentarily see stars. She took the chance to press her attack, punching him repeatedly in the face with her bare fists. She only stopped when Freddy threw fire with his right hand as a quick interruption. When the flames passed and he took a second look, Keishla had disappeared.

"Where did you—AGH!"

Freddy looked down at his stomach, momentarily confused at the dagger protruding out from it. He was bleeding, dribbling blood all the way to the ground. Keishla, behind him, was holding one of her daggers hilt-deep into his back.

She smirked, "Well, looks like your army drained the energy you need to protect yourself from me."

Freddy felt a flash of furious rage burn through him. He

grabbed the tip of the dagger and poured fiery energy through it, burning the weapon to ash. Keishla let go of the handle and jumped away, but Freddy turned into smoke and reappeared directly in front of her. His hands were joined together forming one fist above his head, and he swung hard into the top of Keishla's head. She fell forward, bending in half at the waist, and saw his knee rising to her face. Her head snapped back up and, off balance, she was grabbed by the neck. Freddy threw her body away.

Keishla landed several feet away, rolling to a stop from Freddy's brutal throw. Zenrot heard the sound of her limp body hitting the ground and turned around in time to see her skid to a stop. He ran to her and slid to a stop on his knees, checking her status. His heartbeat was fast.

"Keishla, are you alright? Say something!"

Her eyes were closed, but she was opening them slowly. Keishla coughed and cackled with pleasure. "Yeah, I stabbed the bastard pretty good."

Zenrot started laughing. "Come on, get up." He pulled her up as he stood.

Freddy was slowly walking towards them, holding the wound on his stomach. He started heating his hand, struggling against the pain as it sealed the wound and stopped the bleeding. "Sorry to disappoint you, guys… but you haven't achieved anything at all." He spoke with a smug smirk plastered across his face.

Keishla was annoyed. Even after all the effort she had put into striking Freddy, he looked like he could still fight. Zenrot, holding his sword with his right hand, the blade resting on and over his shoulder, smirked with confidence. "That's not true, Frederick. We just proved you're getting weak."

"And besides…" Keishla followed, "you just wasted a lot of energy summoning that army over and over… It's only a matter of time until you waste almost everything and we kill you easily."

"Like you guys have a chance to begin with. You're just delaying the inevitable. This scythe has more to offer…" Freddy replied. He lifted his scythe, trying to unleash more power. When it looked like it was charging energy and started releasing fire from the blade, however, it exploded. Freddy tries again in a rage. Zenrot watched the scythe not reaching its full potential. He noticed a red dot shining where the blade met the handle of the scythe. It looked like it was Astred's device.

"Something is off…" Zenrot whispered to Keishla.

"What are you talking about?" Keishla asked, confused.

"Before we started our mission to Sentry Run's HQ, Astred was making sure we were ready… and I remember he put a device on Freddy's scythe."

"What about it?"

"Look at it closely," Zenrot whispered as he pointed at the scythe. "Astred said it was to help him balance his energy, but… I think it was to limit his abilities."

Freddy held the scythe out in front of him, staring at it in anger and disbelief. Holding it as a tool rather than a weapon showed him the same thing Keishla and Zenrot had noticed: a small device on the staff at the back of the blade. Freddy charged the scythe once again, watching the red dot shine in real time.

"Bastard!" Freddy yelled in frustration. "No wonder I got exhausted back on our mission!"

"As I thought, Astred knew this would happen."

"About what exactly?" Keishla was more confused than ever.

"Everything. Art Gun's plan. Freddy's betraying us. He knew there was a plan behind them, but my guess is Astred was not completely sure of its details. Even before his death he told me to look after you, but never mentioned Frederick. Now that this has happened, I can see why that night he was busy. He created a gadget to prevent Freddy's abilities from flowing."

"*Mph*. Nice trick, Astred." Keishla answered.

Freddy put his other hand on top at the chip, using all the energy he could draw to burn it. Somehow Astred had found a way for the chip to be difficult to destroy; it was at least fireproof. Freddy's hands glowed, and the fire transitioned into lava. When he removed his hand to check, the chip had melted.

Freddy smirked, moved his scythe into the air, and the blade ignited with an immense fire strong enough to illuminate entire kilometers away from Freddy. The scythe itself started throwing small fireballs around it, almost as if it had a mind of its own. Freddy held it high with a terrifying smile plastered across his face.

"Finally! My real power!" he screamed.

Zenrot, Keishla and the shadow squad were sweating in the increased heat, collectively frightened at what was going to happen next. They were witnessing Freddy's true power: his hair glowed bright enough to light a house, his veins were exposed and visible, leaking heat, and his eyes glowed—they changed color between orange and red, then back again.

Everyone was in position to attack. The fire Revenants burst into dust. Freddy stood alone. He surrounded the battlefield with fire, cutting off any way for anyone to escape. Freddy aimed his scythe at Zenrot and Keishla.

"Now… LET ME SHOW YOU WHAT TRUE HORROR LOOKS LIKE!"

Keishla couldn't wait to see what else Freddy was capable of and decided to attack first. Four daggers lifting off her backpack with telekinesis. They whirled around him, slicing Freddy from every direction, but he was unphased. The knives passed through him as his body turned into smoke just before the sharp edges were able to do damage. He appeared an inch away from Keishla, grabbing her by the neck with one hand. Freddy forced her completely to the ground with raw strength alone. The impact of her back left a series of small cracks in the ground. He released Keishla, lifted his leg and stomping hard on her chest. Her armor bucked around the blow, and the force caused Keishla to cough blood from her mouth. Freddy kicked her in the side, pushing her out of his sight. She rolled several feet away and ended up face down on the ground.

Zenrot, worried, ran to help. Freddy unfortunately was fast enough to intercept him on his way.

"Come on, Zenrot!" Freddy swiped his scythe with his right hand, but Zenrot blocked it with his sword. "Show me you can really fight!" Freddy's left hand started releasing energy, making a fireball, he hit Zenrot directly in the chest.

Freddy took the chance and rushed close to punch Zenrot a couple times, damaging his armor. Zenrot couldn't withstand the heavy blows much longer, so he stabbed his sword into the ground, crouched, and jumped to kick Freddy away. When Zenrot had put enough distance between them, he charged his revolver with his energy to blast Freddy even farther back. Freddy crossed his arms in front of his body to block the shot. Zenrot forced his energy to become stronger.

Keishla was standing up, cleaning blood from her mouth with her arm. She ran over to help Zenrot.

"Is that the best you can do?" Freddy mocked.

"Not quite," Zenrot growled. Keishla attacked with her daggers, but Freddy's fire pushed them away. She positioned herself behind Freddy and punched him hard in the back. Zenrot sheathed his sword, rushed close, and punched Freddy hard in the chest on the left side. Freddy's fire could stop physical combat, so Zenrot and Keishla combined their assault to make sure Freddy didn't get an opportunity to fight back. Overwhelmed, Freddy grew furious and let go of his scythe, turning into smoke.

Zenrot and Keishla were ready for him, but Freddy released a small explosion from his body and pushed them away. He sprinted quickly and grabbed Zenrot by the back of his head with one hand, delivering a vicious headbutt. Zenrot staggered back, disoriented. Keishla reacted to fight back, but Freddy kicked her in the ankle, swapped himself to Keishla's back, and punched her a few more times. Her armor was crushed inwards in several more places before he kicked her away. Zenrot saw Keishla flying his way and grabbed her.

Freddy was brushing dust from his shoulder, staring them down with his glowing orange eyes. Fire still poured off his body to the ground around him.

"What a joke you are…" he stated, his expression threatening. Freddy calmly walked towards his scythe, snatching it from the floor before fixing them with a joyful smile. "Let's see if you guys can survive this." A tornado made of fire rapidly began to form in the air over Freddy's head.

Zenrot and Keishla were amazed and terrified, asking themselves how Freddy was able to use such powerful abilities without any apparent consequence to his body.

"Now… time to di—AGH!"

The tornado vanished. The shadow squad had helped them out, flanking Freddy by throwing grenades behind his back. The fire spreading around protected Freddy from the explosions, but the several concussive blasts broke his focus. The squad started shooting, but the fire kept spreading, consuming the bullets. Freddy was angry at being interrupted. He spins his scythe in circles as he turned around to face the squad.

"How about I get rid of you guys first?" Frederick said, annoyed, then fired a blast from his scythe. The flames coming toward them were so intense that, if they hit the soldiers, they would certainly turn to ash. Zenrot ran fast as he could in front of the squad and blocked the beam of fire with his sword. The weapon was intact, but the armor on his hands started melting. His skin was burning.

"Get out of the way!" he yelled at the squad over his shoulder.

"Yes, sir!" Randell responded as he and the rest of the squad moved away.

Keishla attacked Freddy while Zenrot was recovering. She focused her energy to form and shoot a giant energy arrow—this one passed through the fire and finally made contact. Before she could celebrate, though, he turned into smoke and disappeared.

"Where the hell did he go?" Keishla desperately searched the area, wondering if he had run away. Keishla found him half a battlefield away as he struck the ground with his bare hands, producing an earthquake. He slowly dragged a giant, molten boulder out of the ground; it was bigger than an eight-story building. Keishla sprinted away with her superhuman speed to avoid the attack. As Freddy kicked the boulder with his leg to start it rolling, Keishla realized at the last minute he hadn't been aiming for her—he was aiming at Zenrot. Freddy knew Zenrot had reached his limits from protecting the squad and was making a move to take him out.

Kevin looked at the boulder across the distance, "Zenrot, look out!" he screamed. Zenrot raised his head, seeing the boulder was close but still reacting quickly enough to stop it with his bare hands. The giant boulder kept moving to crush Zenrot. Freddy quickly moved to the right until he could see Zenrot, charging a fireball to strike him down.

Keishla ran forward at massive speed, getting close to Freddy. He lashed out with one leg as she closed in, though, catching her in the face and pushing her back. Freddy completed the fireball and released it toward Zenrot. The fireball was on its way, but Zenrot couldn't let go of the boulder to react without squashing him and the shadow squad.

Randell and his team tried to find a way to help him.

"We have to do something fast, or Zenrot will die!" Daniel said, panicked.

"Any suggestions?" Randell asked his team.

John looked at the boulder. "There is one way…" His tone was tinged with sorrow.

"Isn't there another way?" Robert J. asked sadly. He knew what John had in mind.

"It's either save Zenrot, or we all die!" Arnold shouted to make their decision quickly. Randell acknowledged their choice as they came to a consensus: save Zenrot no matter what happened.

As Zenrot struggled with the giant boulder, he realized the shadow squad was preparing their weapons. "What are you doing?" he yelled. "This is your chance, leave now! You won't have another opportunity!"

"We know, sir," Randell responded. The squad snapped to attention, every man with their hand at their forehead saluting Zenrot. "You and Keishla deserves a good life, sir. Win this fight with all your heart. It has been an honor for us to stand alongside you both."

"What are you talking about?"

"Aim for the boulder!" Randell commanded the squad. Everyone aimed at and shot the boulder to break it into pieces— pieces large enough for Zenrot to take cover from the fireball behind. Keishla found a place to cover herself from the impact, speeding into the ruins of a local market. It had fallen apart, but the walls were good enough for her to protect herself behind. Zenrot looked at the squad shooting at the boulder, finally understanding their intention. Despite the anger he had with them, Zenrot acknowledged their bravery. He didn't want the soldiers to die.

"Stop!" he screamed at them with anguish raw in his voice. "If you guys continue, you will all die!" They cracked enough of the boulder, but it still hadn't broken into pieces. Each man took out a grenade for the final blow.

Kevin chuckled, "We know," in response to Zenrot.

"Don't worry about us," Daniel followed with a smile.

"Despite the fact we couldn't know each other a bit better…" Robert J. started, content in thinking he was doing the right thing though he didn't usually smile or express his feelings openly.

"…it has been a pleasure for all of us, my friend," Arnold finished the thought Robert J. had started.

"THROW THEM NOW!" Randell screamed his last order. They threw their grenades in unison and, when they struck the boulder, all of them exploded. It crumbled around Zenrot, fulfilling their plan to make many rocks fall on top of him to cover him from the fireball. It wasn't much, but they knew Zenrot would survive with all the rocks sheltering him. As the rocks fell on top, Zenrot screamed, an arm outstretched to the soldiers.

"No! Please!" Zenrot lost sight of the squad when the rocks dropped around him. Seconds later, the fireball hit the rocks covering Zenrot in a massive explosion. Fire erupted over the battlefield. Keishla, hiding behind layers of walls, could still feel the fire's intensity. Keishla ran further from the source of the explosion.

Zenrot was under the rocks and could see all the fire spreading through a small hole. He saw as the squad was consumed by the wall of flame, each of them turning to ash.

"NO!" he screamed, his tears evaporating as quickly as they hit his cheek. A few minutes passed and the world had gone quiet. The fire had stopped spreading—everything around was gone. Buildings, houses, debris… all of it. Only flames remained.

"Dark Boy!" Keishla ran her way to his partner's location. When she arrived, she took out stone after stone, and throwed them away. Moments later, she finally manage to take most rock out of Zenrot. He was laying flat on the ground, looking up at the uniform, gray sky, unable to even tell if it was day or night through all the fog and the smoke. Zenrot turned his head, looking to where the squad had been… gone. There was no evidence of their existence.

Zenrot held back the tears while thinking of how many people he had lost on his journey. Anyone who helped Zenrot had been taken away. He slowly stood, turning and punching the ground in anger. He hit it a couple of times hard enough that the ground started to crack. "Damn it! Why?"

Keishla stood up with sorrow and sadness reflected on her face as well. She knew how difficult it was for him to keep losing everyone he cared for. She stretched her hand to help him stand. "Come on. I know it's hard… but this fight isn't over." Zenrot grabbed her hand and stood.

"When will this nightmare end…?" Zenrot said lightly.

Their armor had protected them during the explosion of the fireball, but it was in critical condition. Many spots were sunken in while others were broken entirely. One or two more blasts of energy and they'd be wiped out entirely.

Freddy was walking toward them. The look on his face was deadly serious; he wasn't playing anymore. For all the heat and fire cascading off his body, he was tired from all the energy wasted. Freddy stopped close, standing and watching the pair. Zenrot drew the revolver out of anger and shot at Freddy.

"Foolish… foolish bastards," Freddy said softly. Zenrot stopped shooting. It was pointless. He knew the energy bullets weren't going to work with the fire still around Freddy protecting him.

"Well… we're pretty much fucked, aren't we?" Keishla said, accepting that this could be the end for them.

"As much I hate to say it, yeah… I think this is it." Zenrot replied with a thoroughly exhausted tone. They wouldn't be able to fight much longer. Freddy held the scythe with one hand, hanging it over his shoulders and imbuing the blade with massive amounts of fire.

"You two are persistent," Freddy said with venomous hatred, "but I am tired of this game." Freddy noticed something shining from afar, falling from the sky in their direction. "What the hell is that?"

CHAPTER FIFTEEN

Something landed right in the middle between the battle of Zenrot, Keishla, and Freddy. Everyone took a closer look; it seemed to be a robot made out of junk. All its parts were brown and filled with mud. It didn't look strong like a Spartan or Golem, but Freddy wasn't taking any more chances. "More reinforcements?" he screamed at the robot. "Tell me… how many are coming?" Freddy was tired of anyone interfering with the battle.

The robot had a monitor as a face. It flickered on, showing a black screen with a white line in the center. "JUST ME," it said. The line on the monitor bounced, showing the soundwave of its voice while it replied. It raised its arm, pointing at Freddy. "AND YOU HAVE GONE TOO FAR." It appeared it had been programmed to have a mind of its own.

Zenrot and Keishla were asking themselves what was going on, as they didn't know where the robot had come from. Keishla took a step, approaching it and asking, "Who the hell—"

"Who are you?" Zenrot interrupted, directly addressing the robot.

The robot looked over its shoulder. "A FRIEND." It turned to look at Freddy with no further explanation or information about why it was there.

Freddy ground his teeth in anger. "Identify yourself, Metal Head," he threatened.

"SUCH DISAPPOINTMENT YOU HAVE BECOME, FREDERICK CROSSVELT... LOOK AT YOU... NOTHING BUT A BAD EXAMPLE OF THE MUTANT RACE, AND A BAD EXAMPLE TO YOUR COLLEAGUES."

Freddy smoldered, holding the scythe tight while staring at the robot. He looked like he wanted to destroy every metal part. "For a robot with a mind of its own... you have the dumbest data in your system. You don't think you will get away from here after stepping in like that."

"OF COURSE NOT," the robot responded to Freddy. "I WOULDN'T STAND BY YOUR PERFORMANCE IF I WANTED TO LIVE." The robot stood firmly, then leapt towards Freddy. It raised an arm, about to swing a single punch to his face. Freddy stood firmly, letting the fire surrounding him act as his shield. He was confident the robot wouldn't pass the flame— he figured it would probably melt in the process.

He was wrong.

"Agh!" The robot passed through and punched him straight on the cheek. Freddy was pushed back, blood dripping from his lips.

Zenrot and Keishla were in shock, their eyes wide and

mouths hanging open. Wondering how the robot had easily hit Freddy without any struggle. "He… The robot, hit Freddy?" Keishla spoke, still shocked.

"That robot didn't wipe out the fire, but passed through it. It would have to know his energy so well and engage at the exact right time to hit him," Zenrot responded, still analyzing how it could have succeeded.

Freddy was furious. "It's official, you have a death wish, very well." He hit the ground with the staff of his scythe and smoke began pouring from the blade. It slowly took the form of a living thing: a monster made of smoke and sparks of heat on the inside with burning, orange eyes. This one wasn't like the fire Revenants.

The robot took the chance to throw something to the ground in front of Zenrot and Keishla. "THOSE ARE ADRENALINE SHOTS…" the robot said. "THEY WILL HELP YOU RECOVER SOME OF YOUR LOST ENERGY. IT ISN'T MUCH, BUT HOPEFULLY WILL LAST LONG ENOUGH TO END THIS FIGHT."

"Just who are you? Why are you helping us?" Keishla asked, but the robot didn't answer. Zenrot glanced down to the needles and crouched to grab them. He handed one over to Keishla and quickly stabbed the remaining needle into his thigh. Keishla didn't feel safe using it since they didn't know who the robot was or if he's trustworthy. Zenrot didn't believe they had much choice—either believe the robot or die by Freddy's hand. Turning into ash wasn't an acceptable outcome, so Keishla also stabbed the needle into her thigh.

Freddy's summon turned big enough to block the view of the sky. Standing behind Freddy, the smoky monster was growling in anger; it was as if he shared the same feelings as Freddy. "I will crush you to pieces and burn every single one of them. What makes you think you can defeat me with such crappy parts? You aren't even close to as strong as my energy source!"

"YOU TOY TOO MUCH WITH YOUR ABILITIES. YOU SHOW NO PRIDE FOR ANYONE ELSE BUT YOURSELF, FREDERICK. I THOUGHT I TAUGHT YOU BETTER THAN THAT…" the robot lectured. It wasn't showing any insecurity. It knew this would happen from the very start.

In that last sentence triggered Freddy. He looked over his shoulder and spoke to the smoke monster. "Kill Zenrot and Keishla… I'll handle the robot."

***

The adrenaline seemed to have recovered some of their energy, so Zenrot and Keishla got into position, ready to fight. The monster was getting closer, and they were frightened just by looking at it.

"Oh, come on! This isn't fair…" Keishla said, looking at the monster.

Zenrot spoke through his teeth. "Who would have thought Freddy has this much power…"

Keishla was frustrated watching how the monster kept getting bigger by collecting all the smoke and fog, making itself stronger, "I know right? This is just overdoing it. What is it anyway? Looks like a giant fart," she said sarcastically.

"It doesn't matter… take out your bow and destroy it!" Zenrot shouted at Keishla. The monster growled and started approaching. Zenrot drew his revolver and began shooting his energy bullets, while Keishla shot energy arrows with the knife bow. All their energy passed through the monster, having no apparent effect on it. Both mutants were terrified—if energy couldn't affect the monster, it would be pointless to fight hand to hand.

"Damn it! Our attacks are useless… what do we do?" There was terror in Keishla's voice.

"It seems that Freddy's entire energy source is focused on powering that thing… Run for it!" Zenrot ran in the opposite direction from the monster. Keishla was confused but followed.

The monster raised a hand formed of smoke, a hole opening in his palm. He aimed toward Zenrot and Keishla, shooting small meteors out of the hole.

"Dark Boy, where are we heading?" she yelled to Zenrot in a panic. Both dodged incoming meteors as they ran.

"Somewhere—anywhere!—away from that beast! That thing is immune to our attacks but is obviously consuming a lot of Freddy's energy," Zenrot said, agitated, as they ran from the monster.

"So what? We just run away until it disappears? That's what you're telling me?" She sounded disappointed at Zenrot's failure to think of a better plan.

"Do you have a better idea?" Zenrot shouted at her.

Keishla took a quick look at the smoking monster. "Running away it is." She was grumpy about the situation but recognized there weren't a lot of options, either.

"Besides, he's exhausted as us. This is his last chance to kill us. It won't be long until he shouldn't have any energy left." He tried to give Keishla some hope, even though he himself wasn't sure of the situation. He needed to provide her with a reason to keep fighting.

"I just hope it disappears before it murders us," Keishla muttered. Deep down, she was more frightened than she would have ever guessed she'd feel in a situation like this.

***

Meanwhile, Freddy and the robot were fighting hand to hand. The robot could only defend itself. It appeared to have been designed with a limit to its actions but knew where to strike Freddy. He fought with caution, wondering how the robot knew so much about his abilities. Freddy thought to himself, *"He knows every move and weak point I have—almost like he's known me for a long time. Who is he?"*

***

Zenrot and Keishla were meters away from the monster that's moving at massive speed in their direction. When the smoke hit the ground, Zenrot and Keishla stopped running. More fire Revenants have been summoned.

"Again?!" she shouted, frustrated.

"There aren't as many as before. It appears Freddy's energy is almost at his limit!"

"Still! How much energy can Freddy have?" she screamed, rushing ahead to the Revenants. She wanted to eliminate them before more were summoned.

"Keishla, wait!" Zenrot shouted on his way to help her. The monster stopped him, however, by launching a barrage of meteors at Zenrot. He was forced to run away, dodging them.

More Revenants were summoned on his way. Zenrot took his sword and sliced them while running, trying to save all the energy he could to use his abilities later. He noticed Keishla fighting against the Revenants. She tried to use her telekinesis to lift her daggers, but barely had enough energy to do so. One of the Revenants attacked by surprise and hit her with a flaming punch, pushing her away while falling to the ground. Keishla stood quickly and threw a dagger with her hand, stabbing the Revenant's head before bringing it back with her telekinesis. She fell to her knees, needing rest.

"Keishla!" Zenrot screamed in the distance. "We need to save what's left of our energy—our current weapons are all we have left. Make them count!"

Keishla drew her daggers from her backpack and pushed herself to stand.

"Yeah, yeah… I'm still alive by the way," she said, lightly irritated. Revenants were running fast toward her, but she was holding the daggers and ready to strike. Once they got within range, she sliced their necks and cut the head of four Revenants with a single swipe. The remaining Revenants stopped and stood still. They stared at her, becoming careful in their approach. "All right freaks, here's my offer. I'm going to cut every single one of you so hard that you'll regret coming to this world. Deal?" Keishla was agitated as she spoke to the Revenants. Sweat covered her face and blood colored her hands. Despite her exhausted state, she kept a smile on her face.

***

Freddy moved straight to the robot and punched it in the head, knocking the human-shaped metal body to the floor. He wasn't even struggling to connect his attacks. The robot slowly stood back up and could see it could no longer continue the fight. The robot lifted its left arm, revealing a small label that indicated "self-destruct." It activated it.

Freddy rushed close to attack again, throwing a small amount of fire at the robot. He noticed the robot was not moving; not even trying to defend itself. *"Why doesn't he fight back? Is he running out of energy or something?"* He thought. Freddy didn't delay running within striking range to knock the robot down with his scythe to the chest. The robot was slowly shutting down.

"Gotcha!" Freddy shouted with joy. "You didn't think you would kill me with such basic skills, did you?"

"NOT AT ALL… I NEVER INTENDED TO…" The robot rapidly rebooted, turning itself back on and grabbing the staff portion of the scythe. It pulled itself closer to Freddy. "HOW COULD I POSSIBLY KILL ONE OF MY FRIENDS?"

Freddy was shocked and surprised at what it said. "What— Just— Who the hell are you?"

"I AM HOWEVER…" the robot continued, ignoring Freddy's question, "GIVING THEM A CHANCE TO DEFEAT YOU… ONE CHANCE, AS SMALL AS IT IS… TO WEAKEN ALL YOUR ABILITIES."

"What are you doing? Whatever you have planned, it won't defeat me!" Freddy shouted at the robot, but it only chuckled a small, mechanical laugh in return.

"ZENROT... KEISHLA... FREDERICK... EVEN IF I'M JUST A SMALL COMPILATION OF DATA ... IT WAS NICE TO SEE ALL OF YOU... ONE LAST TIME... FAREWELL," the robot said at a high enough volume for the three of them to hear.

"It can't be... It is you...!" Zenrot shouted. Now he understood everything. The robot went silent, but a beeping sound came from its chest. The noise repeated faster and faster, increasing in speed until the robot's chest opened completely. There was a massive explosion, and Freddy let go of the scythe to cover himself by crossing his arms. The blast damaged the front of Freddy's armor, but it seemed that the intention wasn't to hurt Freddy directly.

The whole area that had previously been on fire and full of gray clouds was no more. The whole area was as cold as a glacier, and it was snowing. The bomb had done something to the surrounding area, flash-freezing the moisture in the air and seeming to have altered the ecosystem in its immediate radius. Freddy's breath clouded in front of his face as he exhaled. It was cold.

"Right..." Keishla said in a long, drawn tone. "The hell was that?"

"One last chance to defeat him..." Zenrot said in a low tone. He quickly took his revolver, pointed it at Freddy, and shot him. Freddy saw the shot coming, whirled his scythe into its path, and blocked it with the blade.

"Oh! His fire shield... is gone!" Keishla said joyfully.

Zenrot followed up quietly, "The robot was an emergency

backup in case Frederick went insane with his abilities, forcing him to lower his energy." Zenrot remembered back when they first met. Arashi had shown Zenrot the file for each mutant, and he remembered Freddy's report, about his weakness: cold temperatures. Zenrot had completely forgotten about Freddy's weakness, but the robot knew about it—and knew this moment was coming. Only one person could have come up with such a backup plan. Astred.

The fight should be easier now, but they were also drained for having already fought for so long. Fortunately, the monster wasn't primarily smoke anymore; it was taking form. Slowly, the smoke was turning into molded, shaped stone. It was taking on a strange shape since the ecosystem changed.

Keishla chuckled, "Well, isn't that handy?" She had a momentary smile on her face, an actual moment of joy. She held her daggers with her hands, lifting one up in front of her face. Freddy seemed worried, but even with his abilities limited he could still fight.

"So? What if my energy has been reduced? Both of you have used too much of yours and can't handle a proper fight. Even together you don't have any hope of defeating me!" Freddy said, taunting them as he sent the huge monster.

The monster throwed a fist at Zenrot and Keishla from above. Both dodged by jumping to the side and the monster hit the ground, instead. Zenrot was located on one side and Keishla on the other. She encountered more Revenants on her side, but the monster itself decided to focus on Zenrot. The monster looked like he couldn't shoot meteors. He was grabbing debris from around him and throwing it at Zenrot.

He ran from the monster, but some Revenants got in the way. He killed them quickly with his sword, swinging until they were in pieces while continuing to run. Zenrot was becoming tired and stopped moving. Fire Revenants closed in around him, and Zenrot shot them with the revolver. It wiped them out, but his energy got weaker, and he had to lower his gun to rest. The monster took the chance and threw a giant portion of debris. Zenrot saw it coming but couldn't keep running. He moved aside, dodging, but when the debris hit the ground a big piece of solid cement hit Zenrot's forehead. He fell to the ground, head bleeding. He was too exhausted to move even a single muscle. Looking up to the sky, he saw the monster holding his hands together, focusing to shoot a strong meteor. Keishla killed all the Revenants, then looked to where Zenrot was. The monster was about to make his final blow.

"ZENROT!" Keishla screamed loudly enough for him to move, but he couldn't do anything. She ran with all her speed to save him. The monster shot his meteor, and Keishla jumped with all her strength to grab Zenrot. They both tumbled away from the attack. Keishla was standing, breathing heavily, and panicked. She was tired and wanted to take a break but was willing to keep fighting. "Don't you dare die on me Zenrot! You hear me?" she yelled. Keishla felt heat at her back; another meteor was coming.

Keishla drew a dagger from her back and threw it straight at the monster's face. It was the only try she had. The dagger grew closer and, surprisingly, stabbed the monster in the cheek.

He stopped charging his next attack.

"What the—" Freddy was so shocked that his words devolved into a scream of primal frustration. "The winter!"

"Oh!" Keishla was impressed she had hurt the monster. "So, it isn't immune anymore…" She turned to Zenrot. "This is our chance! Aim at that smoke fart with your revolver and let's send it straight back to hell!" She shouted, then charged the monster to fight him in close combat.

Zenrot gave a short smile, stood, and took his revolver back out. Aiming at the monster, he muttered, "copy that," and aimed for the legs. Energy bullets blasted them apart and the monster fell, putting his hands to the ground to support himself. Keishla got close enough to the monster to attack, but also got cocky. The monster grabbed her tightly with his right hand; only her head showed outside his grip.

"You dumb fart! Let go of me!" she shouted in agitation, struggling to free herself. Then she laughed at the monster. "Big mistake, holding me."

Getting herself captured had been her plan all along.

Zenrot ran toward the monster while he was distracted, got close to his arm, and cut it down in a single, powerful strike from the sword. The monster screamed in pain. Keishla broke free, and Zenrot fell back. While the monster was struggling, Keishla took the opportunity with her knife bow to slice his other arm many times until it fell apart. She retreated to Zenrot.

The monster couldn't attack anymore; it was unable to move.

"This thing won't last long… and I'm almost out of energy… but they're only one step away from their graves. Better take the chance now," Freddy thought.

Zenrot and Keishla were together, a few feet away from the monster. "Once we finish this creature… Freddy can't summon anymore of his creeps because of his limited energy," he said to Keishla.

"Yeah, but I'm out of energy. I can only fight close now," Keishla said, worried.

"I'm out too… well, let's not waste more time then. Let's finish this thing, once and for all," Zenrot said, sounding motivated.

"Hell yeah!" Keishla replied.

Together they ran toward the monster to finish it. Freddy could see them getting close and capitalized on the moment. He charged his last fireball from his position some distance behind the monster. As Zenrot and Keishla passed within touching distance of the monster, Freddy took the fireball and threw it, forcing past his reduced energy.

"NOW YOU ALL DIE!" Freddy screamed. His intention was to make an explosion large enough to blow them to ashes. Freddy knew he would survive, but at the cost of his armor.

Zenrot saw the fireball colliding with the monster's energy core. He reacted quickly, standing in front of Keishla and covering them with the blade of his sword. It wasn't much but they still had their armor, even if it was already damaged. He hoped it would be enough to survive the explosion. The fireball fully struck the monster's energy, releasing a giant explosion. Freddy was pushed away to one side; Zenrot and Keishla to another. They landed close to each other on the ground. The explosion took a while to dissipate. When it was clear to stand, all the snow had started to melt. The heat of the explosion was intense. Smoke blanketed the battlefield.

A few seconds later, Zenrot slowly stood up. "Keishla, are you still alive?"

She climbed to her feet next to him. "I am, but look… our armor's gone." They stripped the remaining armor pieces attached to them, wearing only their regular MSF uniforms.

"Yeah…" Zenrot said lightly, "one blast from Freddy and we'll be dust for sure." Zenrot started laughing, "By the way," he turned his head to Keishla with a lopsided smile, "you called me by my name for the first time. I'm flattered to know I'm officially a friend."

"*Pfft*… Shut up!" She looked away, and they returned their attention to Freddy in the distance. He was standing with his right hand holding his waist and his scythe in the other. He had been injured in the explosion, but Freddy wasn't thinking of the consequences. He slowly walked to Zenrot and Keishla.

"He seems exhausted," Keishla observed, "even though we haven't fought him directly yet."

"That giant monster he summoned wasn't the best choice. It did force us to our limits, but thanks to the artificial winter it drained his abilities. He should be out of energy by now," Zenrot said to Keishla, holding his sword ready to fight.

Keishla took her knife bow as well, laughing cynically. "I suppose bringing that fart down wasn't a waste after all."

Freddy let go of his waist and charged a small amount of energy in his hand. Zenrot and Keishla took a defensive position, assuming another fireball attack was coming. Using the charged energy, Freddy instead hit the ground, producing a giant cloud of fog so dark they could barely see anything. Keishla threw one of her daggers where Freddy had been standing, the force of the throw cleaning a straight-line path through the fog.

Frederick wasn't there.

"Did he make a run for it?" Keishla asked. In return, she heard footsteps approaching from behind Zenrot. She could vaguely see a shadow getting closer. "Behind you!"

"Where—*AAAGH!*" Zenrot screamed with all the air in his lungs from the pain. It was too late.

"Finally got you…" Freddy said, relieved. He had stabbed Zenrot from behind with his scythe, the tip of the blade going through and protruding out from Zenrot's stomach. He was slowly dragging the blade of the scythe upwards from his stomach to his chest, opening the wound. Blood poured from Zenrot's upper body. He coughed and spit fresh blood from his mouth as well. He tried to lift his sword but couldn't move. His body not cooperating, he let his sword fall to the ground. The world swooned, and he began to fade in and out of consciousness.

"ZENROT!" Keishla screamed with pain in her voice. She ran to help Zenrot as quickly as possible. Freddy waited for her to get close enough, then kicked Keishla hard in the ribs to push her away. She fell to the ground, trying to get up and help but repeatedly falling. The pain was too strong for her to move.

Freddy focused back on Zenrot, leaning close to whisper in his ear. "I would have enjoyed cutting every single part of your body… burning them… and hearing you scream before killing you, my friend. But I don't feel like playing around anymore. It's nothing personal."

Zenrot struggled to lift his head and chuckled, "Let me guess… just business?"

"That's correct," Freddy gave the sharpest of smiles and leaned back, standing fully upright. "Goodbye, Zenrot." Freddy yanked the scythe from Zenrot's chest and, without the support, he fell to his knees for a moment before collapsing entirely to the ground.

"ZENROT! NO! PLEASE DON'T DIE! PLEASE!" Keishla screamed in pain. She called his name repeatedly, but he didn't respond. His eyes were closing. When they finally shut, Zenrot was totally still. He was no longer breathing even shallowly. The gasping, gurgling sound from his struggles to breathe were gone as well.

Freddy turned to face Keishla, casually shaking his scythe to get rid of the blood. "You're the only one left. The only person left knowing my past and who could stop my future." He had an evil look in his eyes and a sick smile on his face as he spoke.

"You bastard! I fucking hate you!" Keishla tried to stand up. "*Ugh!* We were supposed to be friends! We were supposed to come back to the top of the mountain when the war was over; to reunite the three of us! Do we really mean nothing to you?" Keishla fell back to the ground, groaning in pain. She lifted her head, looking at Freddy while holding her injuries with her hand. "Are you going to kill me too?"

"I could kill you right now," he slowly walked over to Keishla, "but it would be a waste of a specimen. You should join me, Keishla."

"The fuck are—*ugh!*—you talking about?"

"You and I are the same, created by humans for their own purposes, but not anymore. We can stop anyone from making anymore creations—abominations! Together neither Art Gun nor anyone else can stop us. The non-mutants believe we're the threat when it's the other way around with their silly experiments. Just think about it, a world of peace for only us." He loomed above her, offering his hand to seal the agreement. "What do you say?" Freddy cocked his head, becoming aware of a strange noise growing louder. He raised his hands and snatched two of Keishla's daggers out of the air, less than a foot from his face. Fiery energy swirled around his hands, and he turned them into ashes. He looked down at Keishla, then sneered and punched her hard across the cheek. "What a shame…"

"*Heh…* you think I would join you after killing my friend? Besides, I'm far different from you. I would never embrace the cruelty you have."

"Trust me, we are not so different." Freddy spoke with certainty. "I'm going to ask you this… Who were you before the war? What do you remember?" Keishla started thinking, remembering having a family. But as she kept thinking deeply, she didn't remember or know who her family was. Her mind went blank.

"That's what I thought…" Freddy grabbed Keishla's hair with one hand and forced her to stand. She screamed in pain from her broken ribs. "Come on! Fight!" Freddy pushed Keishla away, kicking her knife bow across the ground to her feet. "This is your last fight. If you won't join me, at least give me a good show before killing you."

Keishla slowly crouched, her body shaking while picking up the weapon. "I will do everything in my power… spend every last ounce of strength I have left to stop you!"

"That's the spirit…" Freddy said, smiling. He ran to Keishla, swinging with his scythe. Keishla stood firmly and defended herself with the knife bow by parrying his attacks. Her arms were getting numb, however, and every movement was causing pain in her ribs. Freddy capitalized on her weakness and cut across her arms. Keishla screamed in pain, the long slashes bleeding down both her arms. Despite the pain, she kept fighting back.

She reengaged Freddy, swinging the knife bow as aggressively as she could. Not a single strike against Freddy landed. He was able to block every single attack, not even seeming to have to try hard to defend himself. Freddy saw another opportunity and cut Keishla's leg, which forced her to fall to her knee with the other leg. Keishla grabbed her last dagger from her backpack and threw it at Freddy. Freddy took a step to the side and dodged it, then made a few steps closer, swinging his scythe from above to slice Keishla. She dodged backwards, but it wasn't enough. The tip of the scythe blade tore a fresh gash from her chest all the way down to her stomach. Shreds of her shirt fluttered to the side, soaking the blood from the fresh wound.

Freddy circled around with his arms in the air, holding the scythe high again. He swung it rapidly to cut her head, but Keishla threw herself back again. Freddy still managed to catch her with the cutting edge of the weapon, however, and sliced the crease of her left eye.

"AGH!" Keishla slapped her left hand to her eye, trying to stop the bleeding. "You fucking monster! Is that all you've got?" Even now, she still had her signature cockiness.

"That's nothing." Freddy kicked Keishla away. She fell to the ground, rolling near to Zenrot's body. She faced up, and Freddy sat on top of her. He let go of the scythe and made a tight fist. He punches Keishla in the face again, again, and again. He was relentless, not stopping punching Keishla until he became tired.

Her face was filled with blood and bruises. Her eyes were closed and for a moment the battlefield sat in silence. Then Keishla started coughing.

"I'm surprised you're still conscious." Freddy stood, grabbed Keishla under one arm, and dragged her to her feet. Before she could move away or lose her balance, he kicked her in the stomach, rolling her away. Freddy grabbed his scythe from the ground and stalked towards her. "I got to admit… you and Zenrot put up a good fight. The fight of the century… but I'm afraid this is where we part ways." Freddy stood over Keishla once again, looking down at her while stretching his neck and fingers. "Any last words, partner?" Freddy asked gently. Keishla stayed silent, keeping her left hand over her eye to prevent bleeding. "None? Very well…"

The hand over her eye darted up into her hair, fingers wrapping tightly around the hidden knives that had been holding her air up. She dropped her arm and catapulted her hand forward, throwing them straight at Freddy's face as her hair fell loose. He jerked his head back but took one of the blades across his mouth, drawing fresh bleeding lines across his lips.

"Don't you ever call me partner, and I hope you choke on that." Keishla spoke her last words defiantly.

"You bastard!" Freddy snapped, irritated. He lifted the scythe to kill Keishla once and for all but found himself unable to sing it downward. Someone had appeared in the way, holding the staff of the scythe still high in the air. "What the—" Freddy said, scared.

Keishla gasped, surprised and shocked at who was holding the staff. From where she lay on the ground, she could clearly see Zenrot standing slightly behind and off to the side of Freddy.

"Im— Impossible! You're supposed to be dead!" Freddy yelled in desperation. Zenrot pulled Freddy closer and grab him by the neck, squeezing hard enough to break Freddy's focus and cause him to let go of the scythe. Zenrot released a low growl but didn't say anything further. He pushed Freddy roughly to the ground, smacking his head a couple of times before lifting him high into the air. Freddy's legs dangled helplessly, and he started punching Zenrot's arm to free himself. Zenrot threw him away and he landed flatly on the ground. Freddy turned to look Zenrot up and down, a look of confusion spreading across his face as he noticed something strange about him.

"What are you?" Freddy screamed at Zenrot's appearance. His eyes had gone fully dark gray, as if he had been blinded. His skin had developed a pattern of metal spots, and he had visible veins of a silver color.

"That is not Zenrot… What the hell is going on?" Keishla asked herself.

Zenrot stretched his arms, looked up at the sky, and let out a massive scream. It sounded part human and part machine. The polyphonic scream cemented the fact that Zenrot was something else. He started releasing immense amounts of energy, the ground trembling and cracking around him. The wind blew heavily in

Freddy's direction. "This energy… is not his—PROJECT V?" Freddy sounded terrified. He asked himself how he would fight something like that, especially when he was already out of energy.

Zenrot ran unexpectedly fast, almost faster than Keishla's energized speed. "I will not be killed by some dumb science project!" Freddy yelled, holding position to defend himself. Zenrot crashed into him and, in a flash, was punching Freddy in the face. Both fell to the ground with Zenrot landing on top of Freddy. He held him hard by the neck with his left hand, so he won't be able to easily escape. Zenrot balled his fist up tight, his knuckles stretching and creaking. He punched Freddy in the face multiple times, so hard his forehead started bleeding, nose broke, and bruises began developing on his cheeks and eyes. Zenrot was putting a lot of Project V's energy into his fist.

Just as he was about to hit his last blow, Freddy turned into a trail of smoke. He flitted across the ground to Keishla, then collapsed back into his actual body. Freddy spat blood and fell to one knee, looking at Zenrot with a mix of surprise and disappointment on his face.

"What an ending. This must be a joke, to be killed by that thing!" Freddy said, sadly. He chuckled and, despite the damage to his face, managed a brief smile. "Looks like I won't be meeting my goal after all. Before I die…" He searched through a pocket and threw what he found inside to Keishla.

She grabbed it in the air; it was the photo that they had taken a few days before the mission.

"They only had time to make one and—*agh*, Astred gave it

to me. Said it was a token to remind me to think wisely before I made a decision." He winced, the movement causing a fresh gout of blood to pour from the wounds on his face. "He really looked after me, even after my choice was made." Freddy laughed softly. "Astred always was one step ahead of us. It's funny because, instead of being our partner, he was more like our dad." He looked over his shoulder to Keishla. "I'm pretty sure you think the same." Then he fell under the shadow of an approaching Zenrot, slowly advancing on him. "I let my anger and hatred control me… hope you don't do the same. Be better than this— Better than me… I'm sorry."

"I only have one question," Keishla said. "How the hell didn't this picture burn up while you were fighting?"

Freddy choked on the laugh that rose hard from his chest; he couldn't believe that was the first thing that came to her mind.

"Keep that humor alive, you'll need it… well, see you in the next life, Keishla," he said his final words to her. "If I'm going to die like this," he yelled at Zenrot, even though it was honestly more directed at Project V, "I'll at least take you down with me!" Freddy ran toward his scythe, snatching it from the ground and readying it in his hands as he rushed Zenrot. He slashed aggressively with his scythe, cutting all over Zenrot's body. Freddy stabbed Zenrot with the tip of the blade, but Zenrot didn't react or seem to feel any pain.

Zenrot grabbed the staff of the scythe, pulling it while Freddy still held on. He headbutted Freddy hard enough to make him dizzily let go of the scythe. Zenrot held the blade with his left hand, even the cutting edge was razor sharp and cutting him.

Without even a wince, he crumpled the blade into his fist and snapped the staff portion in half across his knee. He hurled it far from the battlefield, then resumed his relentless chase toward Freddy. The other mutant fired very small fireballs from his hands, but they burst against Zenrot without doing any damage. He was running out of options and only one thing was left. It might not kill Zenrot, but it was worth a try. Freddy put his hands on his chest, charging all the energy he had left for the final blow.

Zenrot was getting closer and closer.

As Freddy charged his energy, he thought about his past and his actions. Despite the hatred he had for everyone, and for trying to kill Zenrot and Keishla… at that last moment, he felt truly ashamed. For disappointing Astred. For failing as a friend.

"I'm so sorry, Astred..." Freddy said his final words and, as Zenrot grew close, he exploded himself. The cascade of energy released from Freddy's body caused an enormous explosion, almost reaching to where Keishla lay on the ground.

She only saw the bright light, believing both had been blown to pieces. However, when the light faded away, one was still standing. It was Zenrot, all of his skin burned but healing fast— probably because of Project V's genetic manipulation.

"He's dead… Frederick Crossvelt is dead." Keishla said, shocked at what she had witnessed and shakily standing. Zenrot made a small growl and started running toward Keishla. "Zenrot?" she asked, worried.

Zenrot punched her hard enough to make Keishla fall. "*Agh!* Bastard broke the rest of my ribs!" She screamed in excessive pain, looking up at Zenrot. He just stood still, looking down at her, shuddering as he stared.

At that moment, Keishla knew that Zenrot had the infection, "I know why Project V made those holes in your arms. He wasn't burning you from the inside—he was injecting you with a virus," she said, still laying in the ground. Zenrot rushed toward Keishla and threw a punch from above but missed and hit the ground. Keishla rolled away and staggered desperately away, leaving her knife bow on the floor. Her arms were wrapped around her waist, battling against her pain.

"How long are you going to mess around for, Zenrot?" she screamed in desperation for him to have conscious control over his actions. Zenrot lifted his hand and sprinted to Keishla, swinging his fist in another punch—but attacking much slower than usual. *He's fighting himself.* Keishla had a feeling that Zenrot was still in there somewhere, struggling with Project V. "Zenrot! I know you're in there, snap out of it!" She dodged another of Zenrot's attacks while she tried to find a way to bring his consciousness back. "Listen to me, you bastard," she said aggressively, "after ending hundreds of lives and destroying countless machines… we can finally be free from Art Gun… and you're going to let yourself be taken over by that project shit?"

Zenrot growled in anger, drawing back his fist and hitting Keishla in the face. She put her hands up as she bowed to the ground. Zenrot's revolver fell from the holster, but in his current state he didn't seem to notice—or care.

"You can't even put up a decent fight," Keishla taunted, trying to provoke Zenrot to his senses. She crawled to Zenrot's revolver on the ground; Zenrot walked with his hands down, his back twisted, walking in the opposite direction towards Keishla's knife bow. He crouched to pick it up at the same time Keishla picked the revolver up. She stood by leaning with her left hand on the ground and pushes herself up while steadying the gun on her right arm. Her legs were shaking.

Zenrot started running towards Keishla, holding the knife bow in his right hand and stretched back, ready to swing with all his strength. She lifted her right hand, shaking while holding the gun, and pointed it at Zenrot. Keishla looked at him with genuine sorrow in her eyes.

"I don't want to shoot you, Zenrot." She looked down at the ground, holding herself together and struggling not to succumb to her tears of sadness. He was getting close enough to attack her, holding the knife bow ready to slice her in half. "Please Zenrot, I NEED MY FUCKING PARTNER BACK!" She yelled the last word, emphasizing it with the raw desperation in her voice.

Zenrot had already swiped the knife bow down to cut her head, the tip of the blade abruptly stopping as it touched her neck. Zenrot struggled with himself, fighting the Project V to come back to his senses. He fell to his knees, screaming, and punched the ground many times as he struggled internally. His left eye changed, the gray eye fading and revealing his normal red eye with the black pupil. He gasped a deep breath, on his knees bowing to Keishla.

"Thank you for that…" Zenrot said, agitated.

"Thank goodness, you're back!" Keishla lowered the gun, happy to see Zenrot. He desperately threw the knife bow to her, his face frightened in a way that she had never seen before. The bow fell at her feet.

Zenrot looked into her eyes, breathing hard and in evident pain.

"Now… finish me off, Keishla. Kill me, please!" he yelled. The spot of silver skin on his face was getting bigger.

"What the hell is wrong with you? You just fought off that Project Slimeball and came back, just do it again! Don't be dramatic," she said as a joke. By the way he spoke, though, he seemed serious about his choice. Zenrot held his head with both of his hands, fighting with himself.

"Listen… this thing is already controlling my body and mind," Zenrot said while stretching his arms forward, trying to choke Keishla. After a moment he quickly moved his hands away from her. "I'm struggling just not to kill you right now! So please, finish me already." Zenrot got close to Keishla, crouching to pick her knife bow up and put it in her hand. He wrapped her fingers around it and made her hold it tightly. They stared, eye to eye. "Afterall, you said if we ever became enemies, you are the one who is supposed to cut off my head, right?"

"But—"

"No buts!" he interrupted. "If you don't kill me right now, you'll be dead. And I'll be a mad killer! So please—hurry!"

"It wasn't supposed to end like this." Keishla couldn't look at him in the eyes. She looked away, holding back tears but knowing she must kill Zenrot by force.

"I'm sorry Keishla… but I won't be able to hold it much longer, so please do it quickly."

Keishla pulled her hand back while holding her knife bow,

finding the right angle to decapitate Zenrot with one blow. She was acting tough in front of Zenrot, but even the façade of calmness only existed because she was pushing the entirety of her emotions away in that moment.

"I'm the one who's sorry… see you later, Zenrot," she spoke her last word, holding her weapon high to strike Zenrot, but she couldn't bear to cut off his head. Instead, she stabbed him through the chest, hitting him hard enough to pierce straight through the outside of Zenrot's back. Keishla took a few steps away as Zenrot fell to his knees, closing his eyes and collapsing to the floor. Keishla felt dizziness overwhelm her and fell to the ground beside him.

In the silence of the empty battlefield, it started to rain. A truck approached from the distance, finally stopping close to Zenrot and Keishla's unconscious bodies. From the passenger seat, someone opened the door and got out of the truck.

"Finally, the show is over."

ACKNOWLEDGMENTS

The hardest part for me in writing this series was this specific book. There are so many ways that it could have worked. However, this was the most satisfactory result (at least for me, haha). Don't worry; there's more to come. This is where I started in 2015, sketching with the story, thinking about the conflict and development between these characters in particular. Zenrot will be my primary character, but Keishla, Frederick and Astred were key and important characters in the reaction of each. These four characters never left my mind, and they were some of the inspirations in finishing 'A War for Mutants.'

I want to thank my family, friends and readers all over the world who have been very supportive of the series. This could not be achieved without their help. Whether they help me write this story better or it simply encourages me to never stop writing these stories, and for that, I am eternally grateful.

ABOUT THE AUTHOR

Alberto Cruz Pérez is a Puerto Rican author living in a small house on Trujillo Alto. He spent most of his time on Saturday morning in a library, either writing or drinking a cup of coffee while reading a good book. He has a degree in graphic design, loves video games, and if there's any free time available, he plays a bit of music. Alberto's favorite genres are sci-fi, fantasy, and thriller books.

FOLLOW FOR MORE UPDATES ON SOCIAL MEDIA

WWW.ALBERTOCRUZPEREZ.COM

www.ingramcontent.com/pod-product-compliance
Lightning Source LLC
Chambersburg PA
CBHW020022310726
48970CB00007B/2167